MERCENARIES

Also by John Fraser and published by
AESOP Modern Fiction:

Animal Tales
Behaving Well
Best Friends
Black Masks
Blue Light / Starting Over
The Beach
The Case
Confessions
The Cure
Down from the Stars
The Ends of the Earth
Enterprising Women
Exploring the Clouds
Fake Fur
The Future's Coming Everywhere
Happy Always
Hard Places
An Illusion of Sun
The Magnificent Wurlitzer
Medusa
Military Roads
The Observatory
The Other Shore
People You Will Never Meet
The Red Bird
The Red Tank
Runners
'S'
Short Lives
Sisters
Soft Landing
The Storm
Strangers and Refugees
The Test
Thinking Scientifically
Thirty Years
Three Beauties
Tomorrow the Victory
Unsteady States, Vol. I
Wayfaring
Wisdom

MERCENARIES

John Fraser

AESOP Modern Fiction
Oxford

AESOP Modern Fiction
An imprint of AESOP Publications
Martin Noble Editorial / AESOP
28a Abberbury Road, Oxford OX4 4ES, UK
www.aesopbooks.com

First edition published by AESOP Publications

www.johnfraserfiction.com

A catalogue record of this book is available from the British Library.

First edition 2023, revised 2024

ISBN: 978-1-914938-16-0

CONTENTS

Mercenaries

'I didn't pray,' he says. 'Usually, I pray to the horses, but though they run fast, they've always disappointed me.'

'So, you spite them? With no prayer?' I ask. 'I don't understand. You have work and cash. Why do you bet, resent the losers? You don't need a fortune: but those accumulators would bring you millions, if they ever worked.'

'I have debts,' he says.

'You make debts so that wanting millions seems less mad,' I say: 'Anyway, you've no time to spend on anything but the gamble. Yet, you know how the system operates – you've worked for bookies. You don't need horses, dogs, or anything – it's calculating odds with all the cash that's coming in, to leave the book with profits guaranteed. It isn't racing – it's mathematics.'

'Exactly,' he says. 'It's the beauty. Beauty of the horses, beauty of the odds, beauty of winning – winning more than anyone has ever done.... Like finding all the keys to the great pyramid, intuiting the right order, opening every door – and there's the pharaohs, every one, all alive and waiting for me.'

'You're not mad,' I say. 'Obsessive. An aesthete. Creating – or expecting – the symphony of symphonies, the painting of all paint....'

'The one god,' he says. 'All the other gods' skulls in a necklace round His neck.'

'The Senmurgh,' I say. 'The bird that is a hundred birds.... Whatever anyone seeks, one of everything, one tutti-frutti, one book of books, would be enough.'

'I have company,' he says. 'Comrades. Seekers. The track! Shadows, history; those don't talk, and if we spoke, we'd know we hate each other. Being alive – there is profusion: there's lots are mad and lots who aren't.'

'You're my best friend,' I say. 'We all must have best friends, who don't stand in our world. You drift further, further away – still and always my best friend.'

'Yes,' he says. 'You're lucky to have me. I'm not lucky – as you've said. It's true, there's mathematics to show it all rests on a solid base – but in the end, it's all down to the unknown, the one horse who's quite unaware and changes everything....'

'By winning, if it does. But also – by not winning. Every time – it is identical,' I say. 'Win, lose – it's all up to the horse, but it's the only one involved who doesn't know.... And does it care?'

'Oh yes,' he says. 'But not about me, naturally. That horse is God – at least, His progeny. I'm the benefactor ... the horse is ignorant, but loves to win, like me ... to gratify: life is good, people and horses, they're good too. And happy. Horse and God, He thinks like that.'

'Two independent wills ... and yet, you hope; you cannot will,' I say. He's not interested. 'You're impotent in this – the horse is not. It's up to the animal, who doesn't have a clue what is at stake....'

*

At dawn, a rider comes – on an Electra Glide – bringing the first news: the horses unloaded at the track. Stable gossip. Weather. Guesses and incantations by the sages. All morning, messages arrive – weights, diets, fancies. Who's sick, who's medicated; shoes; who was cast in their box....

'I'll be immortal, if it comes off today,' he says.... 'The capital, to keep the wager doubling up – is quite immense. But if I quit and start again, the level will be so low.... To win'll be a coincidence, not a strategy, project, victory....'

'You'd win a huge amount,' I say. 'Maybe a mention. In print. Not immortality. Going through the card – it is banal: off-days, tracks remote, the weather clement, or quite exceptional ... the time of year.... That's nothing: yours is the coup. But – one miracle, even one immortality – confirms the certainty of death.'

'No,' he says. 'Since Gilgamesh, we know that even in a dream, immortality's not possible. But Gilgamesh shows us – something exceptional can last and last. There must be an arithmetic that registers – the odds, the unconnected runners – and my intuition....'

'Your guessing.' I say. 'It's true, your win would be the coincidence that justifies the record.... Nothing more. The punters, ordinary horses, plus your choice.... The same thing works on fruit machines ... works at Verdun, at Nagasaki: against the odds, someone survives, their number's up, or not. They win. Maybe later, disturbed – they suicide.... There's someone who seems touched by miracles, but it's in a world without a miracle ... there's exceptions for the ordinary, the totally banal ... Surviving, not an immortality....

'It's like us two, alive upon a spinning rock that mostly can't support a life as complicated as ours.... The window of our opportunity is opened – we survive – and then we don't. Our brothers, lookalikes: the same for them. It never happens that by chance a person is immortal, without trying, or being special, charmed, or somehow magicked. In every million, one lives a little longer than the rest ... it has to be. It isn't fun....'

'Well,' he says. 'That was a lot of things you've said! They open up a lot of lives to have, to try to live. There may be a key. Most things – we don't know why they happen, then, we investigate: there's a key. A box is opened to a bigger box, and so, and so....'

'Real life? It's different,' I tell him, though I'm not sure how.

*

I feel useless at the track. I'm not clean, I don't have a brown skin, brown polished knobby eyes, my weight off my back end, thin dainty legs, a midget on my back. The horses – they could be objects from Gabon. They don't walk well, they can't run, obviously, they're grandiose fetishes, two people ill-coordinated parading them sewn up inside – beautiful virgins, I suspect, not like the pantomime men, not at all: delicate boys and girls, all black and bone.

'The runners don't look at you,' I say. 'A punter. They see all these rich mouthy people – they see that they are owned. I think they'd sooner be alone, racing on the sand....'

He doesn't bother answering. A poor grey is gyring round. Greys never win. And since Bucephalus, there haven't been black chargers. And all those mounts that fell in the last century ... shot and shell. Cart horses....

'They should make the owners and their mates race on the track,' I say. 'Look how they're shod! This mud! They'd not make it out the gate....'

'Hush,' says my friend. 'Those loaded old folks make it possible. They own me, their parasite. I'm not worth anything, until I win....'

Of course. Winning gives you worth. You're like your horse – all you can spend your winnings on is horse, more horse. Your dope. All your worth you re-invest – you set it running. You must keep it so, non-stop. They do it all for you – except the win and lose; they're fate and fortune – life in a flash, a pill – down the slope and round the bend and up the incline.

'They all try hard, hard as they can. They have no fault, no sin,' he says. 'You can't trust anybody more than them – they are the pure and innocent.'

'So – what's the difference?' I ask. 'What are you looking for. Some run faster ... and so....'

'So, that's all there is,' he says. 'And now you know.'

*

The third race – we lose. We could go home, but we are already there. It's a disappointment, not a tragedy. We're both quite drunk. It's good, it helps prepare us for the next.

'Listen,' he says. 'Men – and women – you can make from clay. Towers, houses, all the rest, writing – all you know and don't know – all is clay. You walk on it, you bake it – it's you, and all that come after you, the people, towers, houses – writing – everything. But – there's horses. They're not made of clay, not baked in the fire, not dredged up from water, not blood and bones, water and clay. Who made them? What for? Camels, donkeys, mules and yaks – they do the hard work, and if they're not there – men do it – the work. The donkey-work. But horses aren't like that, not for carrying stuff....'

I could object. But – it isn't worth it. God didn't make this, nor anything. So, who did? And why?

I'm convinced. It's an explanation I can believe in, it all follows. Work signifies mortality.

'It's easier to believe you're sick,' I tell him. 'It makes full sense. Addiction to the game. You can be cured, but if you don't want – you needn't be, gambling won't kill you. It's demanding, and you know belief in winning is harder to accept than any other belief – easier to believe in good and evil, freedom and bondage.

'The big win – well, that's something unlikelier than what other people have excogitated. You're a sect, my friend. It costs, it will impoverish you and yours: it may kill them, it won't kill you.'

'It's so,' he says. 'No prophet, no philosopher, no presidents, and no revolution – it needs no line, no wedge, no curve....'

The horses run and run. We couldn't bother less. Let them – they must do it, circle and jump and sweat – bear it all, big midgets, little ones, weights and mud. The whip.

In the train back, he sleeps. I say, 'Those horses. We made them. They are tools. They run like pinballs, or like colours in a pack of cards. Without us to gamble on them, they would disappear – ridden, rendered, eaten, turned into ponies, police accessories, first into dressage, then into reinage, then into broncos; packs, hordes, stampedes, smaller and smaller until – they're gone. Or nearly. Curiosities, but no longer for the track. Short-winded, capricious, barrel-shaped, mule steaks and glue.

'Transformed, you need one for Equus, the Fanciulla del West – but these can be carpentered, or motored by two pairs of human legs, one pair at each end. All ours – made by and for us, discards. Sofa-stuffing. End.'

Friends are exhausting. Incoherent.

*

You can't stop being, having, a best friend. Obsessions, fixations – yours, other people's – they're integral to friendships, any relationship. It isn't good. It's behind us killing almost all the animals, then eating what remains in life-threatening amounts.

Life-saving behaviour – it's a fixation too, it leads to risk, forgetfulness, and lapses of attention – suicide and homicide, of course, like all behaviour, every interaction.

It's exhausting, telling him he's wrong. He has a project – using calculation, reason – to reach unreason, a crazy success. Everyone will scheme, the impossible become commonplace, the unlikely fantastic become – fantastic. Unlikely. My grain is different, modern. I know the solids – people, war, countries – are soluble, splintered, looking down the funnel, the tunnel, of the kaleidoscope at the glass fragments – you shake them, different patterns, entirely ... appear.

'Are they bound to be patterns?' he asks.

No. Only if you keep to your design: perspectives or mirrors? Distances or repetitions?

It's Baltic weather, icy mist: at the track, alone, he made the gesture. He ran out to stop his choice losing in the last race, the decider, culmination ... and the black horse in front killed him. Like the suffragette – and yet wholly unlike. She didn't win, he'd have won all that there is....

If his horse had won, he'd have won the world. So he couldn't keep it. Too big so it was nothing, an 'as you were': a change of name, ownership, of what wasn't ever named or owned.

Winning was so immense it had no meaning. He owned us all, past and present, for ever, responsibility for everything to come. Nothing. Nothing big enough to exchange with, and impossible to shave pieces off all that there is.

If someone beside me had known, they'd have stopped it happening. Instead – he stopped it happening all by himself: the race voided, then his memorial service with no apt texts, only me present.

*

Managing Nazan: the conference centre

If someone loves you, you can tell them; they understand that you know the score. Even if *they* don't. It's a good test. Nazan didn't love me, it was clear – that made me the more frantic. Folly: – but that's where being crazy takes you. It was long ago. Wanting love, from the unlovable.

'We are the only living, edible things left on earth, Nazan,' I say: she smiles. 'Not even armadillos.... People. Only people. We won! We beat all the rest!'

*

She calls me when something happens in her country. 'Country', and 'happens' aren't what I mean, I know real life is not like that. Things are varied, various; there is history, perspective, what you want to see and feel.

I say, 'You are different from me. I am different from you. So, what's the difference?' and we laugh.

When there is repression back there, some manoeuvre, sabotage, a faked election, a hostage ... that's not a country. And the people in it – don't belong to that country, maybe not to anything, not to themselves, that's clear – belong to others, by tradition. Nazan – she feels indifference to me, which means dislike, not admitted, not yet. I'm a pupil – at the most, I'll know what she tells me. It's poor, that: not going beyond what you're told.

'I'm being mobilised, Nazan,' I say. 'We're at war. I'm a soldier, on paper, anyway.'

A dragoon with a shako....

She laughs.

'They made me theirs, back there, by chance,' I say. 'We lived there, then I lived here. I never took the papers here, and no one asked. I'm not from here either, but it's closer, I suppose.'

'Oh,' Nazan says, still laughing. 'I believe you might as well come from here! You've other priorities, of course. People here are xenophobes: so you're dregs. You were for the anti-colonials back there – and now you won't take the step – to fight for them, now they're ... independent. I won't say free....

'And your friend – killed by his obsession ... what a lesson, if we just knew – what about!'

'We all are,' I say. 'Obsessed with staying alive. With eating. Procreation. His fix was winning – like the people who want me as warrior.'

'Just keep quiet,' she says. 'That usually works for everything.'

'If they ask the people here, it will be known – I'm not from here,' I say. 'Or I could claim evolution: I only grew into living alongside them. I don't give up my life to what's been done or not done in my name.'

'They'll send you back,' she says. 'If you make a stir, the most unlikely always want you. You'd have a price. You'd be a case.'

'Advise me, Nazan,' I say. It's desperation.

'I thought you'd like a little friend,' she says. 'To get you off my back. I have a name.... Lettuce. Letizia.'

'You want to find a woman for me, so you can control me more?' I ask. 'It's ridiculous....'

Time is seamless ... it seems seamless, ever inventing itself, using the same characters, the same plots, always new and always recognisable, especially by the stupidest. Colonialism is followed by – produces – post-colonialism. Being drunk leaves – creates – a hangover. Who denies it? You can suffer hangovers, or get drunk again – the hangover creates suffering and abstinence, you may say; or drunkenness and hangovers.

'That's bland,' Nazan says. 'Pointless. You're in a situation – you must decide what to do. Doing nothing is quite complicated.... Consequences? That's the future – by definition unknowable. It'll be you, jumping in again....'

'For me, getting out of things means hectoring,' I say. 'You insisting how you're right, and getting others more gifted to speak and write it down. That's trivial: you're the trigger on a gun: the easiest part to make. That's a shape that any blacksmith makes, a kind of "S" – the rest is engineering. You're not a gun, you can be pulled but don't fire anything.'

'Anything you do,' she says, 'requires you making an identity, if one's not written down or legible on your face. Go,' she shouts, and waves her arms, a scarecrow. 'Sabotage. Resist and organise. Lead, re-construct. Be the new person. Forget this place – you'll never beat the nostalgics and the *fachos*.... You won't like your comrades over there, your new old country. The results will be a desert. Doubt and despair. Answer to the postcard. Try to get into intelligence.... Hope your side lose their war....'

'Wars and massacres,' I say. 'They go on. Everybody knows....'

'Of course they do,' says Nazan. 'We enjoy hurting people. The less feeling we show – the greater is the pleasure. Women must show their pleasure to the men, or fake it. Men don't need show, nor fake.

'Massacres carried out by message and account books – that's the tops. The high-ups get their pleasure so – just shooting people, or whatever knocks them over – that palls.

'Your friend, the inexhaustible, Gabriel – the gambler, who stepped into his myth: he was building a tower. They never make it – heaven looks quite close, you hear the voices, the corks being drawn, all that ... and then – down it goes.

'What will you get, soldier? When you're back there? Will you say you don't enjoy it, soldiering? No good to say – "those beetroot fields full of mines and unexploded stuff – weren't worth the fight". Of course they are! Who cares about the beets?

'You'll have to show you love it: emotion ... tragedy, comradeship, promotions, rules and cleaning stuff. Exciting, boring, heroic, cowardly. You'll have it all. Oh, how I envy you! Service before everything,' she shouts, parades, and waves her little hat: 'Saluting – not the idiot, but the idiot's uniform, his pips! You'll be doing it all day – and I, poor me, I'd look a stupid if I stood up here, and did it now.... Saluting. Sloping arms. Reveille at five to do nothing every day! Looking up – the lark ascending, hark, hark – and bam! A bullet in your eye. How sad! A monument...?'

'Don't go on, Nazan,' I say. 'I have no comment that's not been overused. I don't want deportation or the jail – that's all.'

*

Nazan's habitus – neat streets like twenty years ago, the flat – no book, no picture: imagination has been banned, or maybe she excludes anything that has belonged to other minds than hers. She captures us small animals, a tigress taking prey back to her cubs. There are no cubs. All her rooms are white, the white carpets – a motif of green leaves.

'I came from a society where the rules were written down: the punishments as well,' she says. 'There's no excuse. I managed to work out what the rules are here....'

She has. She follows them or breaks them – the rest of us don't know what they might be. But – she's right, we're not.

'When you come back, a hero,' she says. 'Letizia – Lettuce – will still be here....'

It isn't so, it's probably not so; irrelevant. A normal person wouldn't bother, wouldn't listen. I do, I analyse, take it all in, she's the oracle, the sage. It's a poor destiny I bring in: and Nazan always gives, and gives and waits for thanks, and never lets go what she has given.

*

'You'll have to take the risk,' says Shapur. 'You'll have to go there, clear it up – you can't do it from here. Go there, explain, and take a letter. You are innocent, you'll be believed.'

'Is that what happens?' I asked him. 'You were in the service, ran a consulate, and believed the innocent, the gullible? Everybody good?'

'Good faith,' he says. 'We know who has it, who has not. You can tell, by looking.'

*

'Lett. Call me Letty, that's what I am, a Lett,' she says. Lettuce.

There's a strong physical charge between us. I don't like her, not at all. It is reciprocal.

'There's a strong physical charge between us,' Letty says. 'But I don't like you. It shouldn't be a problem.'

'Besides,' she says. 'You southern guys – you strut and pout: – inside each one there is a little gay, like a gecko, struggling to get out.'

'I understand,' I say. 'The Baltic. You feel freer than the rest of us ... it's natural ... I was born down south – it doesn't make me anything....'

'You must fight, Vadim,' she says. 'Defend. Your place.... It's you. Parents don't give you anything – not until they're dead, at least.'

'I don't see it that way,' I say. 'I don't like hooks, not stuck into my flesh. Countries, those songs....'

'Our country is inside us, in everyone, all of it,' she says.

'Yes, I'm afraid that's so,' I say. 'But I can control myself, and even if I explode – it's just a pop, compared to....'

'All countries have bits that cause you shame,' she says.

'We don't agree on what those bits are,' I say. 'I know it's easier to be a killer than a victim. If I had to choose, I'd kill, I'm sure. Give me the boots, a uniform, the law ... even the cause .... sometimes you die, but more often – you kill. What's inside you? Do you know? What's the litany? Do you forgive yourself for what you are? If you don't, does it make a difference?'

'Oh,' she says. 'It's not just you. And what you don't know – that belongs to everyone.'

'States don't fight so much today,' I say. 'Not modern ones, anyway. The ancient ones still scrap and want to suck in all the rest. But, the script has changed. It's guerrillas, traffickers, separatists ... the pretexts; the old speeches about justice and rectitude – no one credits them today....'

*

'You have a bigger choice,' she says. 'There's push and shove ... states doing what they do. But, you belong, you have the document. What's interesting is how you use your power, or stand up against....'

'Do I have a choice?' I ask. 'Be a hired gun? Protest, be hounded by the cops?

'Let's not think of normal people,' Letty says. 'You are excluded. You look at consequences – look at the motives, the conditions: the beginnings.'

'I could be a country,' I say. 'Invade and massacre, have an empire, be invaded, partitioned, overrun, impoverished, humiliated....'

'A country could be you,' she says. 'That's worse. You'd be more vicious, quicker to act, more desperate, a hired gun, a tart, a gigolò, panhandler, ragpicker, cutpurse, cutthroat, junkie and dealer....'

'I know,' I say. 'Humanity, including me, it's all one. Invention and tricky fingers. Creation is our mirror. Our death wish kills the dodo, our suicide extinguishes a million butterflies.... Hurting others and ourselves – that's our telltale heart at work: our being alive....'

'You're a parasite here,' says Letty. 'An aristo's horse....'

A horse is bigger than you are – Letty's much larger, more solid and muscled than I am:

'This guy – I guess he's Russian, Ukrainian, Georgian ... that owns....' she says, disliking them, disliking me.

'Yes,' I say. 'Out that way. He bought this mansion as an investment: he never comes. I manage everything. I can't do anything, so I tell the others what to do ... weddings, receptions, plotting and mafias, adulteries and hostaging, recruitment of mercenaries; trading of every shape of whore ... scams to make the innocent put money in the future, in space ... scams based on science, based on dreams, based on the rope trick....'

The work is Nazan's gift to us. It's a castle that can disappear at dawn, when the dew burns off.

'Foreign affairs, coupling with aliens, flying beyond time....' I tell Letty, though she already knows.

There has never been a better job. Nor greater shame, if you feel shame.

I'm a Cabral – not sweating to discover Brazil, but having all the tribes, feathered or naked, coming to greet, discover me. All the murders and despoiling concentrated on myself, a singular....

'Don't dare complain,' says Letty. 'Or criticise. You are the principal, the enabler. Victim and guilty.'

'That's true,' I say. 'That's no surprise. Everyone's aware of everything; and who cares, even me, who's a victim.... Victims are hurt, even if they hurt themselves. Being guilty is another way of getting hurt. You're saying I'm hurt twice, a double victim....'

'Some people are bad, worse than others. They must be stopped,' she says.

'Everyone backs all sides in disputes,' I say. 'States and insurgents morph into enemies, or friends. Fight, deal, pay ... abhor, sympathise, negotiate. In the end, states don't fight states: the winning side fears the individual who lurks and plots – the bomber who gets through.

'In your case, Letty – your home, your place, is yours – no one will disturb you. There'd be no profit. Relax. Don't sing.'

'Maybe they'll use a mercenary instead of you,' she says. 'Like the ancient Italians. Lots of fighting, few casualties. The rich lord wins. On it goes – the fortunes circulate....'

'That's sorted many things,' I say. 'The history of the world to come. It leaves me cold ... frigid, frozen.'

'What do you fear?' asks Letty. 'Leaving aside your apprehension – your death in action....'

'The Andes,' I say. 'They terrify me. And the courage of all those who lived on them....'

*

'I always get a conversation wrong,' Letty tells Nazan, thinking of my fear. 'Sometimes people tell the truth, it passes over me like a dark bird chased from a dark wood. I should rejoice when there's sincerity....'

It's quite a stupid thing to say.

'You waste your time,' Nazan tells Letty. 'Think of your spirituality, not of the dank grey home you left so long ago. Think hot and dry.'

'I don't need try,' says Letty. 'Everybody knows how I should look, so that's my way. I don't need change my name when I move around. If Vadim goes back where he was born, he'll have to change the name....'

'Oh,' Nazan says, 'those Russians. They have so few names, they bat them round – you never know who has which one. They all believe the same things, quite exactly. If you have no values, Letty, I could have been your compass. Those give direction, not commands.... Take a trip, find yourself.'

'Yes,' says Letty. 'Magnetism: it's quite useless in saying where you want to go. If you already know, you've no need of compasses....'

'Vadim's stubborn,' says Nazan. 'Shapur told him "get a lawyer" – and he won't.'

It's not true. It's probably immaterial, like the law.

'A Russian name,' Nazan forges on – 'Doesn't even mean you have Russian parents. Or Bulgars. When I was in Cuba, it was full of them. "Defend the Revolution" said the walls – everybody knows, the revolution changes constantly. Chases its tail.

'The thing to ask is – "If you have to go, fight, defend something – what do you choose? Which side? What loyalty? What matters?" Not to you, once you're in it, part of it, on the truck, in the office, the tent, the ditch, the grave.... It's too late, it's too late from the beginning. You are sandhoppers, your head is sand-filled – or you're earthworms and your head is full of mud, you are part of the web, a filament, in your platoon – you can't reflect.... The facts? It's hard to discriminate, and no one lets you. You desert when everyone's been beaten. But – before the beginning – what do you want, what calls you? Principle? Or memory of childhood, a field of flowers, oxen, donkeys, a dragonfly.... What image, what is the last scene, the goal, you contemplate?'

'Independence,' Letty says. 'It's a great thing, if you can have it. I'm independent here. It scares me. I don't have a belief, a job, unless you get them for me, Nazan.'

'Well, first off,' Nazan says. 'You must be independent of politics. They bind you like snakes. If you want work – there's Vadim's place, his position....'

'I don't think he'd keep me on,' says Letty, nervously. 'I'm quite like him – I know what's to be done, and can't do any of it.'

'Then you'd better be the boss, instead of him,' says Nazan. 'When he goes off to do his duty.'

'I read and read,' says Letty, sounding desperate. 'Where does it go? What will become of it? Something or nothing?'

'Oh dear,' says Nazan, laughing wildly. 'You've been sucked in! Language games! all we know of reason, all we can manage of an order, rules and infractions.... That was all the rage a while ago. Where does reality go, if it all depends on language use – and all our rules, if all is rules of syntax, and our vacillating understanding?.... Hand signals? All the lies we have been told.... Machines that speak and write? The new Big Game, invading everyone, no tanks, and no invasion, yet our heads are taken in, and over, surrendered while we sleep and swap our photos with our pals.... Come, my dear – I'll tell you all about the rules ... travel round, go to my hometown ... they won't let you speak or put on lacy underwear, there's quite a different set of rules. Watch out! You won't want a whipping in the street! Some words are brought in from afar, relate to dirty games and stars unspeakable, unwatchable, not on TV or on the social, no backing group or sexy singers, deviants and unbelievers, bad sports and prejudiced.... Let's ask as well: "Are our brains hard-wired – is that a comfort to you, does it answer where your education will lead you to?"'

'I understand all that,' says Letty, close to tears. 'It's all been common coin – even the inventors concede much on this. Language, reality: don't seem to explain a thing, they are conditional, self-invented, conventional, misunderstood and misinterpreted. And rules, dear Nazan: who makes them? Let's suppose they don't fit our circumstances or our consciences ... what then?'

'Well that's too bad, my love,' says Nazan, cuddling Letty, big and strong though she is, unwieldy for embracing ... though ready for a kiss....

'Think of Vadim, and especially his job – a mansion to be rented to all the louche and underhand ... what fun!' Nazan goes on: 'All those retiring rooms with peepholes in the tapestry: the modern world on film, an everlasting "what the butler saw" ... and you, my dear, would be a lady butler at the helm....'

'And will I avoid the rocks?' asks Letty. 'And shall we die – starve, drown – or roast?'

'We always have,' says Nazan. 'Hell was always hot.'

'Work,' Letty says. 'It's not how I see myself, it isn't me. But cash – it's jam you spread out on your life....'

'Well,' Nazan says. 'We could agree on this – your folks have banks.... I know almost all those there have laundries where the cash is cleaned from everywhere it comes, like rusty tankers to Kolkata, or to Senegal – your people tidy up the dirty cash, the wormy notes, corroding gold ... you'll have a grandpa or a cousin with the works ... once, these were ports where Russian pelts were traded, now – you sell the skins of everyone who lives and scrabbles for their daily bread.... I ask for nothing strange or wrong – I'll send equivalents of ermines' tails and beavers' shirts....'

They laugh – there is connivance there, for sure.

*

Letty writes, as she has done since she was twelve – a painless chastisement, an accounting:

> *How I hate my weakness, my desire to make a bond, admit to all the things I hate, the compromise, and even worse, I hate my following my traitor feet, they find a path and on and down I go, betraying my best side or what I'd hoped it was, and hate my pity for the gross, invasive men who have no other way but to impose themselves, dumping their bodies on me, their smell, their lumpy carapaces, their superficiality, ideas scraped off a billboard, the sex alarmed and twitching like a prairie dog alerted from its den, all shapes of men anxious only to degrade, humiliate and call it conquest – and so I make a friend of Nazan who's a calculator, knows exactly how I twist and furl – ingratiates and offers me what she's not got, and I accept, accept a plot, a scandal and disgrace to infiltrate, to squirm inside a situation I don't want, to do things I can't manage, destroying others as the prelude to my own débâcle, and ramp myself up, a valkyrie, to outbid a chancer, dealer, fixer like Vadim, an enemy of his own people, if he could but identify where he belongs and who 'his people' are, now*

laced into a cat's cradle of intrigue and laws and rules that make no sense to anyone, their being all a vestibule to violent death, atrocities, insanity and primitive response to insults misdirected, provocations, international ploys and sales, concessions, quids pro nothing in particular and border fences, tiny armoured cars and model jails with sixty skeletons to share three metres square of sweat and shit, and never see an end to rout or route march, no milestone and no monument, no sign of town with notices of altitude and population, just human quarters in iron baskets where the executioners have hoisted them, and then the fear that I have fantasised, invented all I see, responsible in my flesh and blood every minute for everything invented all the same from nothing but my self-condemning and fastidiousness....

'Pitiful,' Letty says, putting the diary in its drawer.

'Sand,' she says. 'My vocation. I can be a wall against the sand – the hot north wind that blows the dunes against my home, the hot east wind that buries Bucharest, the hot winds that dry the lakes, the scourge, the plague of Mali....

'Africa, Nazan. It calls me....'

'I grew on sand,' says Nazan. 'It was all around. Unless there's wind, it's insignificant, unnoticed. Now – I prefer the asphalt....'

There's a silence.

Nazan says, 'Letty, you're not a goose. Goose get eaten – besides, we're all vegans here. You're a stork – your place, your home, is full of them. Like you, they feel compassion. People prepare nests for them. Storks love their partners and the little ones. You have neither, Letty. They fly to Africa. What do they do there? No one knows, or bothers. Africans have other problems.

'Then the storks fly back. They look for their nests, still full, fuller even, of their compassion.'

'I understand,' says Letty: 'Everywhere, there's suffering....'

'Storks aren't made to confront a suffering,' says Nazan. 'Not of anyone. When I lived on the sand, there were plenty of poor people to be helped. There still are, still there all over.'

'And so?' asks Letty.

'And so, there they all are. Not waiting for me, or for you,' says Nazan. 'And always will be. They have fathers. Fathers do a lot of suffering for them. When the fathers die, it will go on.

'Go to Africa – "traditions must be followed". That's the first lesson. Everybody says it, except the crooks and wise guys. Listen! The sand, you'll find, insists, but it is very quiet. Discreet.'

'It creeps in where it can,' says Letty. 'And stays.'

'Exactly,' Nazan says.

*

'Creeping and staying,' Letty says, brightening up. 'It reminds me of Vadim. A terrible story. His father – he was a general in Honduras – or somewhere like. When he was younger, with two sons left at home, he went to Brazil to scout around. To spy? He went on foot – climbed and climbed, explored – ah! the snakes, the *curare*, shamans and lianas ... on a mountain peak, high above these jungle scenes – there was a luxury hotel. He struggled up, he was exhausted ... they steamed off his boots – the mud had set, solidified.... There remained inside one banknote from his stash, which they didn't steal. They set him on the vertical. In gratitude, he went into their souvenir shop, and bought a splendid knife – machete size, indented with many sets of teeth, signed and tempered, silvery, in a fine case for its display – burnished and sharp ... a present for the birthday of his elder son. And so – he returned home.

'And Vadim, the younger, with a cousin, sneaking round, found the splendid knife – burnt it with acid, blunted it, and finally – they broke it, buried what was left – for spite.

'Vadim, when the raptus passed, was terrified. He knew his father loved his brother, despised him, the younger son.... As the day of celebration approached, Vadim was prostrate with fear – of retribution, death....

'Then, his cousin said – "Courage, Vadim! No Russian kills a drunken man!" And so, Vadim went round the bars, day after day, and crawled home drunk and dirty, contused, every night .... The cousin's story wasn't true, of course. The father was a general, and used to killing anyone, sober or drunk, mad or a pauper, armed or unarmed....'

'Well?' Nazan asks. 'Vadim's alive....'

'His father saw Vadim was a booze-hound. Presumably he'd sold the knife for drink: no vendetta, and no jealousy – just a disgraceful youth. A poor subject, Vadim, that is all. Forget him. The birthday passed. No present. There, the story ends....' says Letty, no more to say.

'Huh!' says Nazan. 'I would say – no father and no brother. There's no trace. Probably no knife, no mountain, no Brazil....'

'Oh Nazan,' Letty says, laughing. 'You're so sceptical. He told a tale against himself....'

'... to show he's a survivor,' Nazan says. 'Betraying those close to him, without reflection. Passionate. A schemer ... cowardly and bold....'

'It's my interpretation,' Letty says. 'All's open to interpretation, naturally ... the interpreters reveal themselves in analysing a tale....'

'Oh Letty,' Nazan says. 'You're so sharp, more cutting than that knife!'

They laugh.

*

You're lucky, Vadim,' says Letty. 'You might be called, called to fight at Armageddon. What a chance! No one would refuse that.'

'Yes, they would,' I say. 'These skirmishes. Everyone wants to describe the end of the world. You can't. You try – it's feeble. You're in it, in the drop, from where you're alive with the rope around – to where you drop, out of sight. It's never the battle that involves you, that's decisive ... it's the talk, that no one listens to, repetitious and interrupted. 'Walk the dog, let's eat, let's fuck, let's do the accounts, let's be Taoists today and run in the rain....' That's what it's all about. It's sharp-edged, a quick charcoal sketch, black trees in mist, the raft full of starving people, leaning into the yellow waves to pull out more starving people ... the summary, conclusion of it all wiped from your screen by a dragon swishing its tail.... It's things going on and on, lifting and declining, as you're on the raft, the waves.... Land ho! You've sighted it – and yet – you're on the land already, and in the sea, in the ice and in the melt, the drought....

'What do you learn from fighting? That you learn nothing.'

'There must be principles,' Letty insists. 'You save lives through lies and degradation – but still, you let people unknown to you, indifferent, soldier on ... have lives you envy or you fear. Choose, Vadim! You produce effects you could not live with – yet some are good, some quite delightful.

'You've betrayed your father. Still, to me, you are a Siegfried – the knight, clad in iron.... You're rotten, I know, maggoty, a brilliant moth consumed by ants – but you're ingenious. You can choose, choose the right side. It's no guarantee, of course. The righteous....'

'No, Letty, it's fear, not justice. I don't have a choice,' I say. 'Except to put on the boots, or go to jail, somewhere.'

Or be a fugitive. That's probably the best.

'Redeem yourself,' she says. 'Be my champion.'

*

'I've helped you, Vadim,' Nazan says. 'You're not an easy case. You know the way to come out well – avoid the jail, enrolment in a state you do not recognise, conscription and humiliation.... Yet, you resist!

'Join the other side – guerrillas, separatists. Build socialism, build a free culture, or a tiny folklore. Help them avoid corruption, internal strife and schism, domination by some bigger state or international alliance, big capital, a deal ... the bombs, the rockets. Smallness attracts, although it is precarious, vulnerable – archaic, even.

'You believe in one big tutti-frutti culture, Vadim: it's a nothing.... You want to criticise, yet to believe stuff that's clearly false. Stiffen up! Take a chance, and be rigorous....'

'I know, Nazan,' I say. 'It would be a gamble. I'd need to think my efforts would prevail over everything I believe in, and am sceptical about ... progress, freedom: "authenticity".... Could I engage – a battle desperate and doomed: a marginal success and new dependency? ... and all for people I don't know, don't trust, who'll probably betray, kill their comrades ... rages paranoiac, decades of lies, privation ... jail, surveillance.... I'm gullible and optimistic. I believe the side I back. But ... there's a limit. I won't follow up my acts of faith by living, transferring, where the faith is a reality, imposed. Some lies I condone – but that's it. I won't live under them.'

'You miss the point,' she says. 'It could make you, put you in history. Change you. Try to construct – you'll see how the lies come easier....'

'It has failed, Nazan,' I say. 'It fails.'

'It's humankind. We'll conquer everything, invent fantastic potions, and make the world unliveable. It's us. Accept it, Vadim,' Nazan says.

The conversation stalls. That's what I want.

*

'I've found someone who will smuggle you, Vadim,' Nazan says. 'His name is Ash. There are so many causes, waiting to be taken up, yours not the priority....'

'Consider consequences, Nazan,' I say. 'Maybe they're not relevant, but do it anyway.'

'You temporise,' she says. 'All consequences and risk analyses can show is that individual lives are very random, and their impact is quite less than zero. So, what you do is quite irrelevant. I'm not sure it even matters much to you – if you survive, in twenty years, you'll dress it up, and live with it. And if you die – who'll care, and who would enter in your skull – now happily available but, unhappily, devoid of brain and, for sure, intention. What you want and what you don't – is carried on by others and by happenstance....'

'The dice?' I say. 'The throw of the dice, still chance, but making differences ... the blanks of the Aurora, the poker title, won with three threes....'

'I think it realistic,' Nazan says. 'To contemplate that we live in the last chapter, that when we die – soon after, the whole world ends. I'm not too sad about it, nor enormously convinced. If it doesn't happen – I'll be dead, and I shan't care, whichever way.... My question is, what I do now – how does it influence this final stage? Not much, Vadim. Not much at all. If you fight or if you flee –'

'Oh, little games, Nazan,' I say. 'The role of individuals in history? I don't believe in world's end anyway. That disbelief's significant, and justified. We shall not disappear, the species – lingers on. It's our detachment from its fate, rejection of what's done and doing ... that's the puzzle. Should we care? Or leave things to free will and the uncertainty? What I do....'

'Is part of this,' she says.

'Self-preservation, Nazan,' I say. 'And fear. Fear of what's to do, and what I can. Not hope. Things go on, changes are made, solutions found, new problems rise. What I do....'

'Is give a call to Ash, and ask his terms. And views, perhaps,' she says.

I persist. 'After our death – it's all a puzzle, that is so. And we are powerless. Is it something we can feel about? Is reproduction the first and last thing that interests? We might feel that our species has done good and bad enough that we can say "It was magnificent and quite disgusting ... what more might we do?" And so – die discontented but quite successful.... All ends, as you have said, dear Nazan, that has a start. And so.... What, in the immediate, shall I do?'

*

Ash knows people – they know, he assures me, but he confesses nothing, for his self-protection.

'It's quite ridiculous,' he says, 'but it's the law, and there are thousands – laws and people moving over frontiers, evaluating sides.... It must be done. It's central – the most important thing you'll ever do: decide! Decide what's to be done to start the procedure, that ends – starts – with you belonging to a small or larger whole.... Your choice – deciding how you measure size in – what? intelligence? It helps you to conceive of what, when you're all gone, your group will have contributed, what will it leave – assuming there is someone left that can determine what's of value, and someone near enough an end, a climacteric, apocalypse – whatever it might be – that gives you or them a perspective.... "End of the world, the species, submersion of dry lands, sentence of destruction, plagues runaway...." Something to use to strike a balance. If that's what they decide. It won't be you, for certain.'

'Oh,' I say, 'It sounds like something I should have a part in, if it's to determine what I do or don't....'

'Imagine it's what people thought about a judgement and an afterlife,' he says. 'We've reached the point where we may have to stop and evaluate our past. Or decide what steps we'll take to go ahead, and add another chapter.... There's now no god we can invent to help our mathematics of the good and bad, the maybe. We are responsible for past and future now. Before our time, some people spent their lives at second guess, and others did the dirty deeds they were to be punished for. We are more circumspect, but not more prescient.

'The end of everything is such a curtain! Is there a "beyond"? Is it a curtain? Maybe a blank canvas, forever blank, all pictures elsewhere having been sketched in, or imagined for our time – not being, not "will be", but been and gone.... We leave a picture gallery, without a visitor ... canvasses all white....'

'Do something, not nothing, Ash,' I say. 'That's what my sponsors tell me.'

'When you land,' he says. 'It will be clear. Clearer, I ought to say. Your status then will be explained....'

*

I don't believe him, not at all. When we land, I'll take the document they issue, and return – back to my work, the 'centre for discussion and assignments'. Affairs of states; and just affairs....

*

'I'm the pilot,' says the lady. 'For me, it's dull and arduous. The flight, the job. For you – it's worse. If I tell you our destination – you won't recognise the name, besides, when there's a mist, they will divert us.

'Take this pill....' and she leans over me, her suit bags out, I see right down, past breasts and navel, down to her knees.

It looks like there's a goblin imprinted on the tab. It must be good – 'Obligatory,' says the pilot, and her scent swells out – wild fennel, bryony – and I'm back among the columbine, the ripple wall, the stucco unicorns: my childhood, where the revelations came and went, unparsed, each sunfilled day ... on the hill, the big house where the rich kids lived.

I ask the guy sat next to me – 'These belts are locked, so we can't move – but why...?'

He's more distinguished, a sophisticate – more than I'll ever be. Frayed clothes, a proof on polymers to correct, I see – 'It's all been costed, that's for sure,' he says. 'Most everything has been: the time you wait, or pace, empty time before you can you decide ... when you sleep or watch the ads ... priced in....'

'I know,' I say. 'But if the flight is long....'

'When you pee your pants,' he says, and laughs. 'Try to enjoy the moment of relief. Don't dwell on the discomfort after....'

'My sponsors will have paid for me,' I say. Who among my friends, and why? Nazan, Shapur, and Letty too? 'I trust my trafficker, of course. He said that when we land, the journey's just begun, I don't need to decide, declare....'

'Of course,' he says. 'We all have traffickers – only the wildest, the most savage beasts aren't trafficked. And they're shot.'

I watch the porno video – the lady pilot is the star. It's all done live, in the alcove where the drinks were once prepared: there's laughter, scuffling ... that pill – it takes me back before desire, before the movies had an END, before what went up must come down ... balloons and kites, ground-nesting birds – up, up, they went, and disappeared ... here they all are, with us in the sky, still high, no sign they will descend.

We land: some bumps. I guess the fragrant lady piloted us down. My years flick past, return to the present – like when a gangster thumbs through a stash of notes, pretending he's checking they are genuine. He doesn't do it for the money: like I don't live with other people for the cash.

It's sad, I'm tearfully sad.

'This is a no man's land,' my neighbour says. 'So, you'll find out nothing – they'll process you. You're free to wander round. Some people flee, go to the rebel side. Others cut a deal. Some are enrolled. Mostly, you're traced. They want expendables, not cases that might cost.'

'Traced?' I say. 'I'm here. I don't need to be traced.'

'The police!' he says. 'The Keystones run the show. We know the cops embody and evoke "ambiguity and derision". They lie. They don't believe you. You lie. It can get tough – you shouldn't ever take the pill and watch the porn. You enjoy yourself too much – it's a mistake.'

'Don't tell me,' I say, suddenly terrified – 'This is a jail, a transit camp. Like in Africa, where they massacre, enslave, deport ... the migrants' fate, I know it all....'

'No, no,' says the guy, informant. 'The wretched have a value; they're for sale. You have none. You might belong somewhere, is all. A country needs souls to live in it, so's it can be. But you're a weight. You're heavy. You, your lookalikes, need work, and paying; you'll need cops and docs; you're dirty, violent – you kill the mountain goats and shit in streams ... you argue, quarrel. You go to war – but then, some will need transport – burial back home. There's prisoners, camps of every sort, and buildings knocked about, and special seats on trams for invalids and mutilates. A country would do better without people, but there's nothing else. The animals and insects – those are mostly dead. People are the winning swarm, even when they play at beggaring their neighbour or at buggering the tots.'

'Your reasoning....' I start, but then I see his red armband: 'You're one of them!' I say. 'You were sat next to me, as if I was a deportee! All I need is an exemption and a document, a certificate that say that what I believe is banal, bland and moderation absolute. I cannot handle dynamite, my feet are flat, my sight is poor.... I'm loyal but cowardly, salute the flag and dodge the draft....'

'The world,' he says, 'is not for us, for none of us. "Pursuit of happiness" – ah yes, that shimmering butterfly no one ever has enticed into their killing-bottle, pinned on cork.... Fear God, fear the invisibles, the germs, the end – but cringe before the state, the meagre rights conceded you....'

'My friend,' I say. 'You are perverse. Of course, I fear my fellow man – but then, there's nothing else but him and her to love....'

‘Don’t reason through,’ he says. ‘It takes you years, and you don’t want to waste the time. You’re wanted where you cannot go, exploited where you hate to stay. Your friends paid for you to leave, you hope you’ll be sent back there....’

‘It’s true,’ I say. ‘I wish that I was pure, but as you say – I’m weak and dirty. I’m not one of yours....’

‘That’s so,’ he says. ‘You’re no use to us – we’re strong and boisterous, and hugger-mugger. You won’t be pleased with us, nor with the rebel side. You’re out of time – pure in thought, which has no substance, dirty in your behaviour.... We had hoped....’

‘My oyster is the world,’ I say. ‘But I have pity for the oyster ... and for the world. Can’t swallow either of them.’

‘Go home!’ he says. ‘Back to your friends.’

And so I do.

It turns out, it’s all about our grandfathers. They prove who we are, or who we ought to be.

I know about the holding pens, the guys who’re lost at sea, and in the fields and deserts, sold, tormented, running, creeping under wire and falling under whips and clubs. I’m none of those. They send me back – it’s weeks and months, but I am back! I’ve thought what I must do, it’s not a mission, doesn’t help who is in need ... no document, of course ... but nonetheless....

*

‘Letty,’ I say, ‘I’m glad for you – you being manager of my old work, the centre; and all within the law. Just tell me – is there a job for me...? I love to be with living things....’

‘There’s gardening,’ she says. ‘I’m puzzled, though. The trees, the grass – they grow without a human help.... What job?’

'It's true,' I say. 'Your epic – The Forests of Lithuania. No gardeners appear. It runs:

'each ancient reach
Is called in hunter's speech
"Jungle".'

'Confusion! Forests or jungles? But forgive me: I know about gardening what you know about managing....'

And so – I'm hired. There's neither forest, nor a jungle. There's prey; no hunters yet.

'Write it all down,' says Letty. 'That's what you gardeners do. You build a little hut from wormy wood, quite windowless, inside you write up grievances and titillations. And if the hunters come, like in the poem, you lie schtum among the spades and forks until they go away and find another prey....'

'I failed the test about religion, everybody does,' I say.

The flight, the questioning – threats over me, like wings.

'They want you strong,' she says. 'Your countrymen. Loyal and good at dance. Or flakey, good at sport.'

'I have a plan....' I say.

*

Nazan stands beside me, and we watch the fireflies signalling like new year lights, on the line of cypresses. How it burns, desire! On and off they flash, even – one falls, flaring, and extinguishes. Excess of wanting, or excess of truth – another, born to flash, remain a bachelor, or jailed? Burned out for sex, or disillusion? Truth – is excess, and usually disappoints. You rarely find it in real life. Who's thrilled by finding out the truth, if there's no prize, no innocent, no guilty – an execution?

'All's turned out well,' says Nazan, holding my limp arm and pressing it against her body. 'The positions are reversed – she takes your job, and you – are a mechanical. Down among the roots. Or should it be – you're an organical?'

She laughs.

'It's classical,' she says: 'All's left to play for – maybe you'll be tops again one day. Poor Letty! It's hard for her to manage now, working for someone else – it isn't her.... She knows she needs me, finding her the trade....'

'Over there,' I say. 'They thought me rubbish. They're intriguers, dark shadows. I see why people join the rebels.'

'Oh no,' she says. 'They're really tough, the rebels are. You wouldn't fit. And anyway – it isn't finished. You're still liable, they'll call again. You are not here nor there. They must have thought you were someone else – yours is a clan name. It carries weight ... but it can mislead. One day, you're under guard, the next – a president. Now, here you are again, more puzzled than before: everything can start from where it was. They test your accent – if it's regional, from where they want to go, enforce the discipline ... you are a suspect, and they keep you where they are.... Your parents – tried to disguise you with that name....'

'It's all turned upside down,' I say. 'Do I have an accent? I can't hear ... I don't have parents: I was born in a school, but wasn't there to learn. And I'm on Letty's staff, without a voice....'

'Just sometimes,' Nazan says. 'History resembles life. Mostly we're not responsible for either. History is where you belong, Vadim. Someone else will write you in to life – a walk-on part ... back to the wings you go, or sometimes down the trap.... They tried to protect you with anonymity from the catastrophe we all are waiting for. Alas....'

*

'It's the mercenaries' weekend,' says Letty, in a fluster. 'There's hunting in the park. We need more trees! Quick, quick! And beds – flowerbeds.... They sleep outside, to toughen up. If you can manage snow, Vadim ... and wolves. The warriors play the deer, a Siberian tiger too, the hunters hunt, all run and in the end – there is a feast. The big boss shoots the biggest stag, and I must find a pot that's huge to seethe it in ... a spit? I spit on all of it, but it's no use – oh, nevermore!'

'The countries all have mercenaries, Letty: they're the new game. They must dress the part, roll over, rut and snarl, die, and in the end, it's resurrection: up they rise!' I say.

'These Russians,' Letty says, 'they're so boisterous. I hope that in the end they don't all weep.... How they attract! So well-dressed, turned out – it makes them easy to recruit, hard to resist. Humanity, Vadim: it makes me cry....'

'There'll be clients too,' I say. 'There'll be a movie. Americans won't come – they have the bases, and the movie stars, but everybody else will come here, cut their deal.... Don't worry – you have soul like them, and like the Russians too. Just tell us what to do – I'll make a forest, rivers and ponds, and morning mist....'

Silva

'It's easy to find fun in us,' says Silva, taking off her little horns, holding them out to show. 'Remember the problematic "concept of intension for a robot"? That's me, that's us, my comrades. It's true, we're robots – slaves with elegance and class, perhaps.... Western slavery was permanent – there's been other kinds more generous, contractual. And as for natural language – we robots seem to work it out quite well. We're understood, all over. We're useful. We deal with conflicts states can not....

'Everything is complex, complicated, if you don't understand it, or can't identify components, set them to some kind of order....'

'I understand all that,' I say. 'I know they bring you in to sort things out – reduce the scale ... reduce the count of victims ... leave the field quite pacified; the targets dead. You're brought in to situations that real hostilities – big wars – would make much worse....

'But – the baroquerie ... the dressing up, bringing the tiger in, the boss....'

'Of course,' she says. 'There's accidents. Sometimes we die. But usually – it is the other guy. And then ... we're paid, we go where the orders say. It's not like armies who massacre and wheel around, then hang about, want power, all that. In that sense – we are robots: yes! You make us to resolve what you cannot. Then – back in our box. It's better that we seem archaic ... we are your tigers and your grouse ... you raise us to be killed. We are your frighteners, expendable....'

'I made the landscape, Silva,' I tell her, proud and wanting to move the subject on – using natural language, naturally. 'It's artifice, but doesn't mean a robot's done it,' and I laugh.

'Shall I see you at the feast?' she asks, whisking her scut, mounting her slender horns, preparing to scamper off....

'The feast for robots is prepared,' I say. 'We iced the vodka, and, since you're cannibals, there'll be humble pie ... you not being quite a fauna, but not exactly a machinery ... you have appetites.'

'I know what I am, what I have to do, and who makes me do it,' Silva says. 'You are corrupted, Vadim, but you're saved by being ingenuous. Your boss, Letty – is corrupt and ignorant. *Her* boss is her corrupter, and yours too. My boss is the boss of everyone: the big corrupter. When you're able to corrupt everyone, it's foolish to say you are corrupt. That one, the head man, is the Creator, God. Creates corruption, let's you be corrupt. We're all in His image – except that I'm a robot. Incorruptible.

'We are firemen, not doctors. We put out your fires. Often a fire is heartening. You'd love to see them rage, destroy. And warm you up. But then we come. It's done: the flames ... they disappear. We don't decide which fires you want us to put out – we're in the cellar, waiting to be called....'

'But you aren't in the cellar, Silva,' I say, not believing, not a word.... 'You're here, in the park, among my trees, the little range of hills I spaded up, the pools I dug....'

'Don't discriminate, my dear,' she says. 'It's true, they deny we're there, or here. Yet – anyone with cash can have a crew like ours.... We're not an army – we are specialists in limiting aggressions.... You won't be enrolled, Vadim, in causes, in armies immense, that rampage everywhere and drop their messages of famine, pestilence, extermination.... You're human and our presence has exempted you.

'With us, the world won't end – we're swift and clean....'

'It's true,' I say. 'I'm thankful and – I'm now a happy gardener, nothing more. I'm a Faust, still sceptical, though....'

'And wrong,' she says. 'You're one of those that sets the fires .... Nature, Vadim. Concentrate on peace, equilibrium.'

'I have a load of wolves coming, Silva,' I say, 'on order....'

'Listen to me, Vadim,' Silva says.

'Now I think,' I say. 'It's been written: "On the incorruptibility of robots". It concludes what makes us human is our venality. The many forms corruption takes – from bureaucratic influence to paying cash, from defence of reputation to promotion of incompetents – are of no concern to them.'

'You're the soft kind, with a vulnerable spot for wolves,' says Silva. 'You might cancel them – we're their match, and they're too easily satisfied. All bluster and circumspection. They prefer dead flesh.'

*

It's easy to make snow. They blow it in quantity, on the mountains.

Silva comes to me, after the banquet. Apotheosis – like the operas, when all the animals return to human selves and ranks.

'How was the stag?' I ask. 'The venison?'

'It was boiled,' she says. 'A disappointment. No magic, and no royalty. Tough, for sure, like mutton broiled....'

The boss has special food, and eats alone: enters for applause and toasts.

'It's left to you, the queasy warriors, to shoot your tigers,' I tell Silva, and we laugh.

The Siberian – too precious to be shot. It's virtually killed, and really shut up in its box.

'Where do the clients want you now?' I ask. 'Africa? North or South?'

There's no response, I say, 'Well, there were no casualties, I guess?'

'We have a special way of counting those,' she says. 'And there was magnificence: the stag of stags. Dead in the fall, rampant in the spring. He went on the fire. They know when it's their day. The stag's the myth: the boss is real. Immortal.

'The bosses – they amass great wealth, a following – harems of every sex and faith. You must have seen the operas. The stags may die, they rise again, the bells go tinkle-tang, quite frantic. There's splendour unimaginable .... The boss remains.'

'And you?' I ask: 'Once there were hordes – now there's just a single load of you, I doubt if you discharge your guns....'

'There's a solution to avoid disasters,' Silva says. 'We'd like to be immortal, all of us – see, how we gambolled in the park that you'd set up – no one was hurt, no wolves, no vultures. Nature, the seasons, the sacred lady singing arias.... It's a masque, a metaphor ... a tribute, even....'

'But there's an enemy,' I say. 'And there's your price.... It's why you are, why you exist.'

'Mostly opponents run away,' she says. 'The fighting part is small. What brings out millions – it's the people, looking for their food, somewhere to sleep, to settle.... How they run! It isn't up to us – we're trained, and so we're few. We aren't the cause of anything – we solve. I told you, we put out the flames....'

'I know,' I say. 'You've told me many times. I'm just the gardener.'

'How do I strike you, Vadim?' Silva asks. 'With horns? Hooves? Tail? What goes best for you...?'

'It's hard to tell, with all your bulky equipment on,' I say. 'Besides, the more people you know, so desire grows less. I can't discriminate.'

'That's the opposite of what we're taught,' she says, looking at me, coy. 'Family happiness. We're more sociable, of course. My parents were Armenian, I'm Russian. Maybe a relationship's worth striking up....'

What to say? Tell something about Letty, or the ones who do her work? Foist Silva off? You can't do that to anyone....

I say, 'I'm full of streams and hedgerows ... everything seems a past, layered; frilly parasols, spaniels, porcelain cups.' I make it up. Everything, it's true, seems to have happened before, without the lies and manoeuvres, without Nazan.

'You could come with us,' she says. 'Write it up, exonerate us, show the human side. Get us business. Show how we're always in the right, or do our best.'

'The garden – it's a universe. In the beginning, someone had to mow and tidy. It's been so for every civilisation. First the gardener, after, the proprietor,' I say.

'I have a man,' she says. 'He's perfect, we understand each other, my – how he suits! But – I'd like to try something a little different. Difficult.'

'Oh,' I say. 'It palls. Like the caviar diet – you end up puking.'

'The state,' she insists. 'All states, having the monopoly of force, create and then extend the oppression that is the destiny of all the wretched of the earth.'

'You are a part of it,' I say. 'The state. Those myths you play out ... a charade....'

'You're quite mechanical, Vadim,' she says. 'The states are all responsible, for everything there is. Militias, guerrillas – their ambition is to form a state. The single party, with its boss: the state incarnate. Can't you imagine a different force, an independence that changes the scenario? That the wretched can refer to ... their champion....'

'I've often tried,' I say. 'But you're not it. I'm sure. There's many, different things to try, but mercenaries aren't one of them....'

'I'm sceptical, my friend,' she says. 'You don't seem bothered by the fate awaiting humankind – not just the roasts and floods – but the great increase in the dispossessed, the "never-hads". New unclaimed masses, expelled, unregistered, unnamed, unarmed, trudging directionless....

'So, you plant some trees, Vadim, and you forget the rest – the millions wandering the earth, sheltering, succumbing, surrendering....'

'I don't forget,' I say. 'My trivial history – so complicated and obscure – unexplained and unresolved.... I couldn't take on more complexity and dependency ... lost in an endless forest of conifers, identical....'

'History is like that,' she says. 'It's not meant to mean something, and you're never typical of anything. Imagine. Think! This place, the house, the park. If only it wasn't Letty. She doesn't run it – her memory of you, that is her guide.

'Think deeper – Russians are at home with Russians. Siberia has melted into mud. Where is left to go to? The South? Kazakhs and Chechens? It doesn't fit.

'Years ago, the Poles, Hungarians – they were a picket fence, not something you would trust or suffer for.

'There must be other ways – I've shown you one. This could be our place....'

I think of Letty – her cold, wooded home: – a part of her, she said. Do you believe all this? What they say, who they are, where they want to be? I don't believe a word from Silva, the more she talks, the less I am deceived.

I want to be in charge again, get rid of Letty. Everyone who works here knows what they must do. It won't depend on me. Still ... over it all, there'd always be Nazan....

'See how it goes with Letty,' I tell Silva. 'All the rest – it's unbelievable.'

I remember – there were those revolutionary Lettish riflemen, a century ago. Where did they all finish up? ... the Russian colonists in Central Asia – partners, guides, instructors? ... Russia was always home ... always is, wherever people go, end up.

'It doesn't cost you, to go along with me,' Silva says. 'You've no place now – just earth and saplings. In the world, you've seen it for yourself, there's no good side to join with. Distributing food and drugs? – they wouldn't take you. You've crime up your sleeve....'

We laugh. I suspect she's right.

*

'No, absolutely not,' Nazan says. 'No mercenaries, not from anywhere, not claiming independence or that they're soft missionaries. They're messengers of despair, Vadim, and provocation. Your old job – that we can fix: – but soldiers on a squat! The park a fortress? No, absolutely not.'

'Sort it all out, Nazan,' I say. 'Silva is different, maybe she'll stay – but all the rest's an ad, I'm sure.'

'All of you is waste,' says Nazan, quite angry now: 'Credulous, incompetent. Greedy and ill-informed. Outside, there's millions more capable than you....'

Silva replaces Letty? Or maybe not

'Letty's reserved,' Nazan says, 'but she'll resent having Silva set over her. Beside her. Silva's strong, not stubborn. They won't say she's a deserter. "Seconded" it's called. Suspendel cand. She'll do the military side....'

'There wasn't one,' I say. 'And me?'

'Oh, you'll have all the rest,' says Nazan, with determination. 'Don't take orders – do what's required, that's all. Have a romance. Either of the women – if you're straight. If not – fish for yourself....'

'It's of no consequence to me,' I say. 'I'm dismasted, bouncing on the careless waves. Is this what having life entails? Something intimate, they say, that should be each one's goal, that's more significant than war and peace, or crime, redemption.... Not work, position, persecution, but satisfactions that can justify, compensate, our flaws, our pettiness. Is it important, having a home and living in it?'

'I'm not the one to ask,' says Nazan. 'Homes fall down. They're left, deserted. You'll need an address to put on forms. You need a status: "married, pending, dead". You need these things, it's formal, naturally – no one cares.'

'Silva says – these dispossessed – *they* care. The family, the house, land, animals.... You mustn't lose them, when you do, you're a vagabond. A mercenary,' I say.

'You want a parade to join. Or be a character in a famous book, Vadim,' says Nazan. 'It's false, it's not for you. Fix the park. If you can't, tell someone under you to do it. Take the credit, take the blame.' She gathers height. 'Talking of blame – it's you that's soft on our neutrality. Spies, lax judgements – those are your specialities. How many times I've heard you say, that you could live in China. Be content. Even in Los Angeles.... You must decide. Are you for civilisation, or for yourself? Even dear Silva, who we've let into our hearts, our payroll too – she may be a spy, or have false nationality, or sympathies....'

'It's quite unfair,' I say. 'I have no platform to stand on, to defend myself....'

'Oh,' she says. 'Don't exaggerate. No one is interested in your views – it's your character that is at fault. Perversity. Survivalism – you'd do anything to live an easy life....'

'You may be right, Nazan,' I say. 'Letty's ingenuous. So am I. We thought all orders came from you....'

'There are no orders anymore,' she says. 'That was the colonial tone. Now, you must make up everything yourselves, and take the rap when it goes wrong.'

'I don't know which is worse, Nazan,' I say. 'When you controlled everything; or when you have no power at all.'

*

Nothing, no one, anywhere, compels you to tell the truth. Nor to be urbane, moderate in reactions, sober in plans.

I have a mercenary, Silva, ready for use, with no regard for truth, but keen on striking up alliances. My rage at Nazan. The perfect customers.... And the pavid Letty, has no link to general prejudice. I could engage Silva to eliminate them both as she thinks reasonable, discreet. I need no justification, no defence, since I'll not be accused. Anger – my motivation. They distort my life, present and future, work, enjoyment.

I don't hire Silva. She is my rusty pistol in the drawer: my trusty pistol. Evolution tells humans to use anger to combat greed and ambition. Survival. Evolution also tells us not to do anything, not to make things worse. I try to forget my anger. Too big for me?

*

'Gardening,' says Nazan, 'belongs with patriarchy and racism. It's a menace. No animals and so much waste – bring Vadim indoors, let nature take his space. Leave him out there and he will suffocate us: cutting, burning, setting traps and mowing grass.'

'People sell stuff to people who are like them,' Letty says. 'We'll fill the place – cops love selling stuff to cops. Soldiers to soldiers – they're insatiable, and mostly won't be used, or won't go off bang, or even phutt. The perfect customers ... And diplomats – exchange of gifts drives them like coach-horses....'

Nazan interrupts. 'And I am nearer my objective. A Greater Syria. It's talked about, but then it's dropped: resolve the Syria question, throw in Lebanon, Iraq and Jordan too – and that's the start.

'You children – Letty, Vadim – you don't know how commerce works, still less how drawing up the map you want can make us rich and comfortable....'

'Your name, Nazan,' Letty exclaims.... 'It all brings lustre to your name....'

'No, no, it's not for me,' Nazan shouts. 'It's the beginning. The Arab universe.... Nothing to do with me – indeed, it is the contrary – but so, it starts small, and takes in Africa....'

'I don't feel I'm with you....' Letty says.

'You must understand,' says Nazan. 'We are all Arabs – all, at the beginning. Some remain so, others forget. Nonetheless, it's everyone's condition. Once nomad warriors, now sedentary – we fidget and we itch. Where is our home, who are we, why the despotism…? All the wretched, the accomplices, those who've lost the fight, without the language and the faith, potentially, that's all of us ... we see our commonality receding; bleeping like the aliens in other galaxies.... All of us, seeking the unity, the confusion which is within all unities.... The universe a buzz of energy, like you leave something on, no sound, no picture, but the will, determination – that goes on....'

'More conferences?' I ask.

'For a start,' she says. 'You must agree – the vision is magnificent.'

'I feel I'm marginal,' I say. 'To all big plans. I'm used to living in other peoples' projects and trying to get out.... There's China, archipelagoes and atolls – a line of wants, desires and certainties, and other geographies as well.... You ought to spoon those in....'

'Your gambling friend,' says Letty. 'What does his life tell us? What moral comes from him?'

'A life lived for success, not happiness or conformity – he came as close to winning as it's possible,' I say.

'A life lived to escape, like yours?' asks Letty. 'How might that end, what satisfaction...? This meeting place, our mansion where we work – it is the frame. The people who come here and talk, and frolic in the wilderness – is that what you would like to be? One of those whose portrait's painted, left on the wall?'

'No,' I say. 'I've no ambition ... after the first few seconds – the walls left behind, the comrades, the projects – just to feel the air, the earth turning away from under my scampering feet...! That's the summit: for me, it is a destiny. A life lived to escape, you call it – what matters is the moment of escape itself. That's all, more than enough – not planting frontiers, designing flags, and all the rest. Just myself ... naked and irresponsible, I fear.'

Not a prison, not a camp, liberated: nor one of either built.

'I understand hazard,' Letty says. 'The rest is puff.'

'You'll enjoy Zelinda,' Nazan says. 'She's the new head of our security – no one undesirable gets in, or out.'

'You put some places in, Nazan,' I say. 'Your outline of a plan. But left some others out....'

'Discretion, Vadim,' Nazan says. 'Apprehension. Taste....'

'Zelinda,' Letty asks. 'Should we do our travelling before she comes?'

'Silva stays,' says Nazan. 'I'm working on her, to reduce her fee. She is my guarantee that Zelinda won't spoil my plans. Silva is the counter-weight.'

'I used to have a plan,' I say. 'No one seemed interested.'

They don't seem interested now: plans get very small....

*

'I told you, Nazan,' Letty says: she tries to weep, but – strangers! However hard we try, we never get out tears for them. On Letty goes: 'You should have given Silva what you brought Zelinda in to do. Now, Zelinda is gunned down by Silva's accident, her spat, her calculus. Her dread. Business will collapse, we'll all be ruined.... A death brings out emotions – violence too. Hate and sorrow – no one spends when those are in their heads.... A mercenary needs business: she has no natural enemies....'

'Zelinda left a note,' says Nazan. 'Unusual, I know. When you are murdered, usually it's the cops that write your epitaph – suicide gives a scope for literature.... Some people make their reputation so.... Read it, Vadim, give an opinion....'

'What does Silva say?' I ask.

'Nothing,' Silva says. 'Why should I say anything?'

'It makes you reflect,' says Nazan. 'We've always attracted rich people. But why should they bother about things? Let's host the poor. Poor people drift and run, it's true: but sometimes they will turn and fight.'

'Zelinda writes,' I begin. '"*I lie out in the wilderness. Many many people have been left here, looking for a place to sleep – like me. It's peopled like Virginia was – the naked and the dying, the robbers and the children ... I'll secure them all, guard them, and all the animals – such curiosity, careless and defenceless, such hunger. Creeping, chirping: brewing curare, climbing like the capuchins. Just – a day breaks, the sun is hot, the balance holds ... and then, for certain, everything will find the instant, break up: they'll move, assault the others, everything living, everything that can, astral, planetary, grebes and okapis ... with the darkness, everything feels free again ... in movement....*"'

'Look!' says Silva. 'Not a mark on her. It happens so – on waking. You're not there, that's all. Big animals, and the otters, anything that just extinguishes itself, unfeeling, unconnected fragments ... a species, a family ... peoples that you didn't give a name to. Extinct. Dead. The first soldiers who turn to farming and end staked out like they are nailed on doors....'

'Well,' says Nazan, 'I'm not sure we're more secure, now that she's gone. Zelinda didn't cost. It's a lesson. Things disappear – it's enough, to have a wilderness, lie down in it. She knew it was a continent, full of anyone, one of many Americas there were, turning vicious, so you hope you don't wake up. Nothing to do with sadness. It's the wild. Knowing it. Vadim can make another garden from the wilderness – it will bury all of us. Zelinda just lay down, and then it shook and shivered her perspective ... she finished there.... Had no idea what she was to guard, or what it fed on.

'Like my plan. It's shaky; that, I see. The Arabs – "all from Adam, and Adam is from dust...." Everyone emerges: we multiply we die. Does it matter how? I've seen big animals – in the morning, they don't arise.... Putting together a hydra- headed people: language, faith, backsliding and variousness: what was never separate. It seems vanity....'

'She lies there,' Letty says. 'Why should we tell anyone?'

So we don't.

She was a handsome woman: – she had marksman's eyes. Feet well-turned – could do the ghost-walk or quadrilles indifferently. Insightful writing. I paste her memorial in the Visitors' book. Visitor is apt! We laugh.

'She must have come from Rum,' says Nazan. 'There's been lots – eternal cities drowned and buried. Romes. Everyone knows who we are, who I am – but no one can find the spot we came from. It was all set out when we got here, like Vadim's garden.

Of course, we may have changed the language on our way. That would be confusion! You know who you are because of the people around who speak like you.... And isn't that a paradox?'

We're all too shaken up to respond to this. It's true: we saw the stag killed, skinned and cooked, but Zelinda, lying on some boughs, eyes quizzing up, the feet raised, but there's no flow of blood to charge the brain – nothing sentient to ask what's next. Zelinda – took it all in – small and large, vegan and carnivore, slavers, enslaved. You can't do more than that....

It's not the way a diva lies – the hands are folded – was she an ascetic? No, probably not. She didn't pray, no faith, no future – she didn't believe in that. Just – security, that she could never guarantee. She must have told a fib to get the job – 'I'll see you through, give you protection – won't cost you guys a cent....'

'She was a sacred liar,' Nazan says. 'They are venerable, they sparkle, you must value them. I don't know why. I can't believe she died for us.... She had no insurance – that's good, it wouldn't serve.'

'She was an exquisite,' Letty says. 'That kind – doesn't last. But, of course, I honour her, like anyone, who dies alone, illuminated.'

'Come on, you chancers,' Silva shouts. 'Stop your inventions! Leave her! She's someone's food....'

'I know you're innocent, Silva,' says Nazan. 'You have your motive, pressing, strong: what do you plan to do with it?'

*

'Nazan's pursuit of empire,' I say. 'I'm not into that. It's fool's gold. There's no place in it for you, Letty. Nor me and Silva – it's a fraud. This platform we rent out – in the end, someone would use it for their big plan, I knew.'

'There'd be room for us,' says Letty. 'All empires co-opt strangers to run them and expand. That's the point – no one is a foreigner. Or sometimes they're all foreigners – French, Italian, German, British, Spanish, Portugese – the parasites. Russians, Chinese – and those Malians! Selling stuff and hoarding gold.

'Americans all over. Empires everywhere, mushrooms: poison, forgotten, fried, marching and hopping, growing overnight. It's an opening: something for us, transforming us, Vadim. Best to be inside, not waiting for the chop, the chip on the document.... You know about that, Vadim! Belonging, knowing who you are, and having it recorded. It will wash Silva clean, straighten you up, and I'll not feel inadequate.'

'Instead,' I say, 'you'll *be* inadequate. That empire won't be a tribal confederation, made of mud and straw, the wonder of the little-known and spacious worlds. It will be another despotism with documents and secrets. Spies and fences. A prison that's set up to scrape the sky.'

'Of course,' says Letty, coming off the boil. 'It's Nazan, so it's business. Cornering resources. Taking over Silva, protecting her, exposing us, you and me, Vadim. We could run: start a farm for animals too old for us to eat. Imagine seeing them, joyful and at rest. Gratitude – a tepid emotion, but maybe that's what is left for us – no victories, no purges ... no heroes and no enemies.

'We're like those people in a first movie, with three figures, acting out a Waterloo, a jerky parting of the waves.... Or a dead scene, like those two bearded connoisseurs, looking down on modernity. The train beneath the iron bridge they stand on – in a moment, they'll disappear in smoke and steam, for ever....'

'We're the servants, bearers, the mutes,' I say. 'The people who come here – their action is killing, killing unknown multitudes ... giving and withholding cash, setting a price, giving a licence, buying food, creating famines ... selling guns, welcoming panjandrums, censuring and conniving. That's their job: killing. Sometimes – people survive, thanks to them, despite them – but the art, gift, talent of the boss – is killing. Cash – is a sideline. They will kill us last, because we fawn on them and serve them.'

'If you're right, Vadim, even as a rant – you're no use to anything,' says Letty. 'You've gone beyond. Banality – but no use. We're in clans – we need a leader, everybody does.'

*

'Everything here was put together by itinerant, uncontracted labour. Each of us is a private company, unconnected with anybody else and their opinions.'

We print this on cards, hand them to the clients; it isn't relevant. We're all sinners, guilty – now or later. It frees us to do almost anything. Silva and I – we leave Letty, the uncertain: and Nazan the manipulator.

'Take a break, you two,' Nazan tells us: Silva and me. 'Silva has this murder rap, and you, Vadim – are son and father of a crowd of holy fools. There's no job here – your garden is a wilderness. Out, out! You two – I expel you both! Come back when you repent, or when you're moribund.... Learn Bambara, Silva, stick it on the other tongues that wag inside your head.... Away with you! Go!'

And that we do.

There is an ad – 'strong workers wanted in a hot and inhospitable spot....'

*

Silva and I join a party of prospectors for a rare-earth deposit we can mine. We didn't know we should take our boots off at night. It's always very hot. We both have problems with our feet, we hobble. She hugs mc in her sleep – it makes us hotter still.

'We're following the future, Silva,' I assure her. 'This is the chosen path – we have to keep it smooth, and hope there's a destination.'

'There's destinations for everything that starts,' she says.

She's glum. We drill, we dig, we ask around – all's gossip, all's a gamble. I'm back in the horses' world ... my dead friend ... arithmetic and racing plates.... I'd settle for a camel, but we're in rusty trucks, and in our boots.

I miss Letty. I miss the good bits. I miss the rhetoric – that's all there was. I miss it.

*

'What's in the tent?' I ask Jair: 'We drill, you're spacing out.'

'Nothing,' he says: 'I'm leader, so I plan.'

'I plan too, Jair,' I say. He turns his back.

'It's chemistry,' says Silva. 'He doesn't like you, Vadim. You are a Northerner – you don't fit in.'

'I could convert,' I say. 'Just tell me how.'

I peek in. There's a box, on the earth floor. 'The little chemist', pictured on the lid. There's pipettes and crucibles. A smell we all could make, when we were very young.

'Jair is certain he can make anything,' says Silva. 'Air and water. Probably, all the rest. We're headed to the future – don't look back, and don't complain. It's useless, obscurantist. He'll take our spadefuls, make the samples an abundance. That is the plan....

'Like chemistry came from alchemy – he plans to make everything we will use come from his chemistry set. Something out of nothing, Vadim. We set up the future – he invents what we need to get there....'

She's convinced. The end of digging. Everything brewed up from nothing, or from nothing much: from banality to eternity ... digging to infinity. Those bearded Parisians, forever scrutinising fresh modernities ... they're us, our avatars.

*

'You're scenery,' Jair says. 'You diggers and sifters. The guys come, like you two orphans, thinking you are finding gold. Your comrades trample you – but all the while, we who seek palladium, have found a new mineral – epithalladium, let's say. That's how it works. Everything, the universe, is ready-made and left for us. All you need do is be ingenious. Look under every bush, in every nest. Some stuff you won't find ever – but there's a creator who must have loved a novelty, surprise – like Fabergé, who left his goods concealed under the roses in Tsarskoe Selo.... Happy Easter everyone!'

As he explains, there comes a shout: 'Here! Here! It's treasure!'

Mohamed, seeking the dust, the source of everything – instead ... finds gold, the end of everyone.

'We're rich?' asks Silva.

'No,' I say. 'We were, when we were digging in the dust. We had a value and potential – we might have found a mass of rarity, a vein down to the centre of the earth.... They'd take it from us: now they'll take the gold. There's danger here, Silva. There's a lesson for all mercenaries. If you take cash to defend someone or yourself – you sell yourself for good....'

'You're intolerable,' she shouts, and I pull her after me. I take Jair's box, his chemicals ... we might need to brew some plastic flip-flops, make a boat, titanium oars, some rain – even a river, or a sea ... create a barren continent, sterile, with nothing anybody wants, a Saturn or a Pluto....

'That was life, Vadim – what you threw away,' she says, 'The gold back there.'

'You're compromised,' I say. 'Silva – I saved what could be saved of you.'

'I'll string along,' she says. 'You are familiar. I'll be credited with saving you ... perhaps....'

We've saved each other. What banality!

*

> 'Before I could count, I hardly knew what reason was....Reason must obey the science ...'
>
> Gaston Bachelard, *La philosophie du non*

'There has never been a rich goldminer, Silva,' I tell her. 'It's true, everything is there, waiting to be discovered. That's it. Once it's discovered, there is science, then reason follows.

'It goes on and on. Wealth isn't part of this.... Gold will never have its science, its reasoning is flawed....'

'Of course it is,' she shouts. 'Gold and little telephones – they won't save the world! – a million, though, would preserve me, even you....'

'Then there's Nazan,' I say. 'Like gold – she isn't reasonable, nor scientific....'

Silva starts to form an answer. But I'm right. She stops.

'It's not just the dust,' I say. 'It's being shut in – the mine. *Mina* – the kind that explodes, the *grisou,* what *grisaille*! – the glum gloom: the power of air, the blast. The mine: the *me,* what I am, what I belong to and belongs to me....'

Silva stares at me. 'We're small,' I say. 'Of course, everything is linked, and what each loses is their life, "what's mine".'

'That's language,' Silva says. 'I know – it binds us. If we don't speak – each one is dead.'

'It's being shut in, enclosed,' I say. 'It terrifies me. In the mine. Me and mine – it seems secure, but you are easy found. The cops. They say your dog has shat on someone's flower. You have no dog. There is no flower. And when they take you in, there's no way to get out, no law, no protocol – it's all a question of the door. How to get out. There's no procedure that will open it, not ever. It starts like that ... it ends like that. For you, Silva, it's worse. You're innocent, of course – but Zelinda's dead, they'll want to hear you, to confess your ignorance.... They'll follow you for ever, till they're satisfied and you are not.'

*

We run and trot – our tension grows, a touch of fear, though the word is out – 'gold' sends crowds towards us, over against us, a mass in oily clothes, and in white robes with staves – all hastening towards the hole.... We find a kind of bothy, like the marsh Arabs used, before the sand took over.... Before the marsh there was a lake. Before the lake – a river. After the marsh – thin grazing. After that – the sand.

'They'll think you are a communist, Vadim,' says Silva. 'I know you are, a sort of one, a subversive. Never sated.

'This bothy was once a refuge for herdsmen, now ... it's our last haven. How we are reduced!'

‘For us,’ I say. ‘My stance – is always what you’d call “philosophical”. Common ownership’s essential, equality we’re born to, and fraternity –’

‘Is an illusion,’ says Silva, sharply. ‘Folly. At a time when philosophy is moribund or dry as chipboard, you’ve contrived to put yourself outside all reason, beyond even true communism and its liberal twists.... You renounce all friendship, hated by all sides....’

‘It’s true, I could be judged a productivist,’ I say. ‘I repent, I know the criticism – but you can’t have famines all the time, and people stuck in villages.... True, sucking nature dry, making duff stuff and being alienated, destroying the earth ... lots of choices lie there, not made ... produce, exploit – how can you not?

‘Humans never wanted welfare, not for everyone....’

‘The factories, the guns....’ she says. ‘Yes, it all sticks together, a taffy of a new confinement, eternal, evolutionary.... You wanted continuity, Vadim, you and your mates ... you used history, the past, as your springboard for the future ... and so off we go! on the ride to the abyss....’

‘Let’s keep off that track, and hope there is a bypass,’ I say. ‘There are just wars and wars by accident and wars inevitable.... The future’s chosen in a general way, and we all follow on, a host of black and piebald sheep ... we seem identical, the bells are tuned different, that’s all....’

‘If you’re a mercenary,’ Silva says, ‘Don’t ever give your nationality. They’ll think your government has sent you.’

*

We’re hungry. In the hut, there’s caterpillars. ‘Maybe they are food,’ says Silva. ‘A touch of famine, and we’ll find our minds, our tastes, have broadened.’

‘They’ll taste of custard cream,’ I say. ‘I never fancied that. I prefer the hatch: the colours, and the drunken flights....’

A face peers in, familiar....

‘That gold,’ says Jimjar. ‘No one said it was in ingots. We thought it was a mine – instead, it was a stash. Belongs to someone else. What disappointment! Everybody yelled and cried – and that was that. All done. Some guys in uniform carried everything away.’

‘And the crew?’ asks Silva.

‘Angered,’ Jimjar says. ‘And someone’d stole the chemistry set. We didn’t know where to start. We rented horses, and now we’re looking for some trouble.’

‘I’ll hop on behind you,’ Silva says. ‘I don’t weigh anything....’ And off they go.

*

Eventually, I find them all – they’re in the largest hut.

‘We’ll try diplomacy,’ Silva says. ‘Having them pay to make us go away. We drove some people off – the little gardens, most are now a wilderness, just like back home. They say that elephants, where they lived, could trample and destroy like that. It’s fair – they had our labour and the gold....’

The head guy, who’s there to cut the deal, looks quite distressed.

‘We’ll find another guy who’s more clued up,’ our mate Jimjar says, ‘If we don’t do this quick. Then we’ll put on a show, and race these horses....’

And that is what we do.

*

'They had little,' says Jair, as we jog away. 'The race will stimulate them. They made lots of bets, so some will have made enough to clear the wilderness we left.'

'This part of the continent,' Mohamed says – 'You won't find cultivation. It takes water, it takes peace, and confidence. The wilderness – all green and juicy, you see melons growing out, like it was centuries ago. Just leave it, and it sprouts. Trash the flowers – they are inedible.'

'Vadim makes a lovely wilderness,' says Silva, joshing him along. 'It's gardening on its head. People come from everywhere to see the green and yellow, the beasts come back you haven't seen since when we tried to poison everything that crawled. A little patience, forbearance – it comes back. Stronger than before.' She turns to me. 'Nazan was right – order comes from chaos. How would she know?'

She's gathering height, she starts to hector. 'We're not enlightened persons, Mohamed, whatever you've been told, we don't use reason, don't shape it into those machines. We're symbolic animals – we think in terms of plums and cherries, of mysteries and things divine and inexplicable, a juicy nature, free, productive, all the year. Symbols: we draw them on the walls and paint them on our heads....'

'We're fruit machines,' Mahomed says, laughing and doubling up. 'Pull our handle – we bring you luck or misery.... Inside each one of us, there is a fortune, waiting for its moment....'

We trade the horses for a truck.

I tell Silva, 'This talk of wilderness brings them back to me: Nazan and Letty, all the intrigues, and beguiling delegations with a promise of the green. "Arab" – for sure, a symbol. There's Arab in each one of us. Unity – the primary symbol: the golden section, the boy in the rope trick who goes up whole to heaven, falls down dismembered. The universe as a whole starts up, the fruit of will and love – some purpose quite inscrutable ... and then it's broken, into pebbles and methane, wandering in a void....'

'You must accept,' Silva says. 'We can't forget, we can't revise, the shapes that's lodged inside us from the start. Tales told and programmed in our brains.... A wilderness that comes before the garden, disorder that underlies all orders ... we build our tales upon the wilderness, where it began, where we were born, conceived ... and in disorder lies all that we live on; and in the tangle – is our food!

'Who thought of that? Who tells the stories, stuffs them in our heads? No one, I guess. It takes a "no one" to plan chaos, extinction of our minds enshrined in compost. Behold! peaches and caterpillars! Food, Vadim! It's magic. Anyone can grow what grows unheeding, whether to eat or rot: – not reason, science – those are not the end, the plan and purpose. Minds grow from the compost like they're aubergines, turn the good earth to dust, dust into Adam, Adam into dust.... Uproot the garden, make the wilderness, and you have a banquet. Kill the stag – you have a feast!

'When people see the wilderness, Vadim, the one you made – no one will think of you. They don't care, not a bit, who was creator of the jungle and its slouching beasts, its wriggle and its creep. They see what could be a unity ... starting in destruction, arising ... plenty and splendour – falling back ... Regression is how life begins, Vadim. Where else can plenty start?

'Order is death, my dear. Time limited and timed to end. Order is empire – then comes its fall, the fall of everyone, conquerors and slaves, the end of everything and everyone. And then it's up! Again. Maybe.

'You won't be there, Vadim. But you could believe it's so. Perhaps one day all will be really done and terminated. That second law; the energy expended, not replaced: but when?'

She laughs, goes on: 'Not yet. The wilderness is home for everyone – no hierarchy, no one decides, no good and evil, all's good and evil, all together.... A habitat before we start to test who's stronger, quicker than the rest. Before we start to kill – everything we can. Everyone...!'

'We've heard all this before,' I say, but I am shaken. This sandy stretch, I wonder – is this a primal wilderness?... Mind? Mined? Does mind come first, create, destroy? Or is it mud and dust? And Silva? Shall we both or singly make the trek back to the exploiter, Nazan, to Letty the self-doubter...? Nazan doesn't know what it is she does. She wins; that's good enough. No one knows what they have done, are doing, it's not necessary. Nazan schemes, her plot is part of the big automaton, the Plot, plots are what earth is made of ... a plot you plant things in.

'Anyway, you're wrong,' I go on. 'The wilderness is not a symbol, not a station on a circle – *I* was the gardener, *I* made the wilderness.'

'Just so,' she says. 'No one has made such a big wilderness before.'

Her riff's exhausted both of us ....

We're out of gas. It's natural – no gas stations hereabouts. We trudge along – too bad we let the horses go....

*

We're happy, all together, all ex-miners, maybe we have struck it rich.

'How do you know all this?' I ask Silva. 'Life, death and rocks?'

'It comes with being mercenary. Trained to bring order, leaving a chaos,' she says, laughing loud.

'It's all true,' says Jair, leaning over, eavesdropping. 'Once there was one world – a huge globe.

'Every shape, design, all modes of life, enjoyment too. All migrating, seeking their best spot, a paradise there maybe was. Then came the day, the explosion – everything flew apart. And went on flying.... It's the universe. Will it come together? Will it hit a wall, go on a swerve, a curve, and find its unity again? Or must we bring in mercenaries?'

He laughs. In fact, we're all in good spirits, on a roll, we prospectors, who've found what will serve our needs – more convenient than what we might have found by digging in the ground.

'The people here are the most intelligent, the finest featured, like we all might have been, until we became monstrosities,' he says. 'They're too intelligent to fight. That's why they paid up, and now I'll share out what they gave, when we reach a tranquil spot....'

I ask, 'By the way, before I got there, did you see, was anybody hurt?' He turns away. Silva responds –

'People are used to it,' she says. 'You have to pay – especially in an isolated place. You pay the cops, then pay the guys the cops send ... maybe they are cops from somewhere else. They use the law, a tax unpaid, or anything at all.... You have to pay, and in the end you always pay or else you leave, expelled, or someone's killed to make the point or just to let off steam....

'Besides, I wasn't there.'

'And nor was I,' I say. 'But there is trouble, I suspect, there always is. Some people do things clean – like Nazan ... with her in charge, there is no blood, no one complains aloud ... instead, us! – we improvise, we guess....'

'There's bands of bandits all around,' says Silva. 'If we don't find the wealth that's underground – we take what's in the houses, in the banks. And, naturally, we have our principles. There's few who don't. We all have something we would like to see. For us – it's honesty, prosperity, unselfishness, an end to cops and despotisms, intolerance and persecutions....'

'But you're a mercenary, Silva,' I remind her.... 'That comes first....'

'Well,' she says, 'a mercenary? And aren't we all. From time to time. It all depends, depends on ends. Priorities....'

'I accept that I'm a bandit, I just want to start off clean,' I say.

That would be in the Sahel, with the Polisario Front. It will never be.

*

'You don't know anything, Vadim, because no one tells you,' Silva says. She's irritated.

'Go further, Silva,' I tell her.

'You won't find out about the guys, the others in the band,' she says. 'They tell you stories, but not because they fear you and your opinions – because they think that you're outside their world.'

'That I don't count, don't care – what do they do when I am out of sight? It's why I don't want to be involved with them.' I say.

'Stories true, false, and partly so,' she says. 'To compromise you, intimidate – or from pride or shame. You're not on their team, and don't have the courage or commitment to speak out. Not that they want that – it's trouble. If you kill people, you don't want trouble about it. But – you're not here or there.'

'And where are you, Silva?' I ask.

'I'm on the team,' she says. 'I'm a mercenary, like you say.'

I never decide – does she mean that, straight? ... or are there other layers, meanings, where she wishes that what there's been, was not? You're always what you do, but some of it is locked away. Possibly, there's something you can do, to correct what's happened. It's all about the telling, not the happening. You must accept that. What interests me is filtered out, something else is written down or spoken, and that is the basis of all judgements. It makes me furious. A fraud. Leave it to the market, like they say...? She's right – I don't really know, no one has told me. I can guess, though, what happens – anyone can make a guess.

*

Being a bandit, or any sort of criminal – the good part is, no one expects you to have ID.

We go back. Silva does security, despite Zelinda. I wait for orders, thanks to Silva.

Pan-Arabism's full of cash and time. Nazan is pleased. I've long forgotten once I nearly loved her.

'We may be witnesses,' Silva says. 'And go back further and be held in court.'

I make myself a nest, deep in the wilderness. The birds don't feed me – Letty does.

An ordinary life: on a bed of bones, the dead unknown; laid out by ancestors, and by me. I feed the animals – though they can do it for themselves.

'Slouched here,' Nazan says to me. 'I'd high hopes of you. You fell, instead. Another mission – that might freshen you....'

'Marocco? That's where I'd start,' I say. 'And move on quick....'

'And there's a new companion,' Nazan says – 'Jalelah. The finger of suspicion doesn't point at her, but many other fingers do.'

Jalelah is determined, forceful. Supple, synchronised. 'Listen, Vadim, I'd not have thought of you as one to travel with or do intrigues,' she says. 'But you'll fit in. I have a plan.... I dance. I'm soloist. But not so well. Yes, the male gaze – I know all that. What I can do – is my big compromise. That's my ambition: study, work the little centres – then I'd see. I need a manager, someone....'

She leaves me in the air.

'We're fixers, Jalelah,' I say. 'On a mission. You dance in your own time. Maybe we would need a strong-arm with us – someone like Silva....'

'Oh, Silva's much too grown up for either of us,' Jalelah says. 'Besides, she's putrid. Before we go, we'll clean you up, and maybe I would tip off Intelligence she's here....'

'We didn't save each other's life,' I say. 'But certainly, Silva and I – we trod a heap of sand together....'

'You're wrong,' she says. 'You forgive everyone except yourself. She'd do us down – best stop her before she has a chance....'

'Nazan wants us further South,' I say. 'Your idea – it's a betrayal in a way....'

'Oh, no one's ever won a thing in history,' she says. 'Snippy-snip – the gossip! Even if you're conqueror of everything. Dance takes you out of that – an audience puts their imagination on a pair of skis – then down the slope and over the horizon. I turn them on....'

'I'm sure you do,' I say. Best say no more, so everything that follows will surprise.

'You know, Vadim,' Jalelah says, putting her right hand in my left jacket pocket. 'Think a little. This project of uniting Arabs – even more than they already are. Have you thought it through?'

'It's a project, books and blood about it, they've flowed like fountains. It's a given – I have never thought....' I say.

'The Turks – got near,' she says. 'There. That's it. Non-Arabs – they unite the Arabs, if anybody can. Arabs who want – unite. What brings it further on – formalities, empires – all that stuff ... it's people who aren't Arabs, or it's despots. It becomes a prison-house. I have a better thought.... Think of those Pan-Slav conferences, the pan-Germans, the anglophones, the francophones ... and let's not mention the religions, and all the troubles those can give.... All gone, too boring, self-evident, or vicious ... horrible and genocidal....'

'The tickets, Jalelah, are for Rabat,' I interrupt. 'There's your career to think of, then my paradise in waiting, the Sahel.... Except – Nazan wants surrender – a peace one-sided, almost certainly false, and I don't want to be her emissary, using my honesty to set bad bargains.... Honestly – it isn't even honesty, just rhetoric....'

'You know,' she says, pinching me quite hard. 'We might not go, and say we did.

'Nazan talks to despots, they're her donors. And besides – artistic dancing is a stony field. There's Yolande and Lola – they're wild beasts with their competitors; they were the tops. And after all – I'm not that good. A life spent coming in at second best – it wouldn't suit. Instead – in other places, they don't know what's what – there's space. People forget. I'd be a memory for expats, of where they were: a novelty for all the rest.'

'You'd have to write – as if from Africa....' I say, set aback: 'Invent.... Before the Sahel gets too hot....'

'My written Arabic is not so good,' she says. 'And those Maroccans – they say they speak the best, the most correct, but I find it hard to understand....'

'And the dancing?' I ask.

'Oh,' she says. 'Much more expressive than the writing. More universal than the opera.'

'And Nazan?' I ask. 'How were you acquired?'

'She took a shine, I think it's called,' says Jalelah. 'In a city, like this one, people like me are the molecule in a pill: a cure.... Up on a stage, my body calls out to slumping flesh and bones – "restore" it says, "your youth and elasticity"; we flit, cajole, inspire ... quick as silver, perfect as sardines.... Remember – there's those of us who've been displaced, and lose parts of themselves; the world of letters and of faith.... It fades away. There's continents all overlaid – there's Arabs in South Iran, then there's the Yemen, its fearful wars; all over everywhere, the language and the faith, the changing notion of a nationhood there's never been and never been forgot.... I am one of those.... Holy warriors: the guardians. The special ones. A sceptic, backslider: me myself.

'You can't call it a diaspora: remember, "the sea of India and China, in whose depths are pearls and ambergris".... Navigation presupposes universes; trade exchanges good, not goods.... Everyone is everywhere, Vadim. I hope you're not a literalist, that thinks a word is universal, like the light, the time, the space – that there's a thing nailed on, belonging to each word....'

'Where did you think of being, Jalelah?' I ask. 'Do you dance in clubs...? And Nazan...?'

'I thought of Normandy,' she says. 'The apples and the cows. And there's the sea.... I might be a new Bardot ... seduced, abandoned, talented.... You're Vadim – too good a coincidence to lose....'

'Why should I cover for you, Jalelah, and risk...?' I ask.

'You always do,' she says, putting her face close to mine. 'What do you risk? Whatever happens, you are set firm in your skeleton until you drop – to end up somewhere in the universe where there's just a scum of souls, like fish eggs, frog spawn, waiting for re-birth, and then you'll swim or hop – up unknown streams, and risk and frolic till you drop, your soul peels off your useless bones ... maybe you start in an acid lake on Jupiter.... You play your luck. That is your gift. Your hope. You risk what has no substance, risk to lose what you must win, to win what you must lose. The world's a wheel – it spins, there's slots, the colours, numbers, you go round and round and give a fortune here, a disappointment there. The bounding clatter of the banal, the ball-bearing dropped in and spun – that's you, Vadim. You feel the force – and yet the wheel's rim is too high to have you spill and roll and bounce downstairs, and find another star, lie in its heat beneath the peach tree, and the pomegranate bush.... Free and confined, that's you. And me...!

'You! The architect of nation, faith, calligraphy? Nazan's champion and messenger? Absurd! Reflect! Be realistic, rational. You have reason: and there's no science that can build on you.... You are plasm, Vadim, just like me ... a gel....'

We cling together, and we weep.

Our universe is small, and closed.

*

Paris.

Jalelah's a liar who always tells the truth. At night she hugs me, just like Silva did. She's cold, we both get chilled. It's terribly cold. We walk to warm our feet, pause on the bridges where they threw Algerians off. Now, there's golden statues everywhere, like in Skopje.

'Silva says we're all mercenaries,' says Jalelah. 'But we are very short of ready. Cashing in the tickets – brilliant. I could ask Letty – but she has nothing.'

'For Letty,' I say, sad and curious for her. 'Her psyche. Cash would be a cure. Not for us, though....'

'Cash, lots of it – Capital – it took the place of other things, long long ago,' says Jalelah. 'Once there were goats and days of work. Then there came cash – the more you have, the less you need to tend your goats and dig. It's natural we cleave to it. Doling it out, manuring it – it makes you old, but not through your exertion. Look at Nazan. She pays to have her wrinkles ironed ... they come through giving orders....'

'If it's not cure, and doesn't gratify, the more we have we leave it when we die....' I say. 'Then why....'

'It must be that we think it gets us things,' she says. 'If you don't think that, you must be mad, they say. Your gambling friend – what did he want? A game, some stupid horses, an obsession – took over from his good and bad.... We all did moral autonomy at school, it means we make a judgement for ourselves, approximate, but no check-in with God! Well, Vadim: what's the answer for your friend – you gave a tribute to him, he had love, if not understanding.... Until he might have won, of course....'

'The game – it covered everything,' I say. 'So, was he after cash? Or did he want to win?'

'It's like "what Arabs want",' she says. 'Someone gets cash, for offering a prize. Nazan for sure. Not me.'

We leave it there. We're cold, and it's complex, and gets more tangled as we talk.

'You need the cash to buy the goats and land to keep them on,' she says. 'Of course.' It doesn't satisfy us.

We don't go on.

'Do you like goats anyway?' she asks.

Paris is tough: you must be intolerant and tolerant. You must be comfortable with opposites. In Paris, you must be Parisian. 'The opposite of white,' Jalelah says, 'is white. Of black – is black.'

I'm sure she's right. There's reason here, all round: and much that's not. It's hard to find some work.

Jalelah does auditions in the clubs. The worse you are at dancing, the more sexy, scrumptious, you appear. You don't get work at dancing, but you get what you don't want.

'I'd do better with the mind,' says Jalelah. 'Psychiatry. Desire: too much, too little, off-road, on the edge. The cure is the disease. You could be my maid, Vadim: open the door, prepare the couch, and lay the clients down.'

'We've fallen off the maps,' I say. 'Nazan will wonder where we are and....'

I don't know what follows that.

*

I ask Letty. She replies, but sends no cash.

'Letty says we are suspected,' I tell Jalelah. 'Nazan thinks we're talking to the wrong kind of Arabs, absolutely. "Those two are in my pay," says Nazan. "They have to do just as I say. They mustn't plot."'

'Oh,' says Jalelah, 'she's smart! But, you know, I plot all the time. I move around, pay cash, don't remember birthdays – not of anyone. I know people here – they don't want what Nazan wants.... It'll never happen anyway, not in any way. We should leave, Vadim. Normandy! Calvados – it makes my stomach ache. And there's the wind and waves.... Maybe we should stay? Go to

Brazil? Or Panama? – I leave it up to you, I've the deciding vote....'

'We mustn't leave, we'll have to ford the rivers, take canoes, go through the jungle, be raped and robbed and kidnapped,' I say. 'We must stay, Jalelah. It's hard here, everywhere else is hard, much harder....' I am terrified.

I go on. 'We have a project that is geopolitical. We're builders. If you can't dance, I'll harvest souls. And I know significant Arabs....'

'They've been thrown out, escaped, run away – they're worse off than us. It's true they've all been ministers and presidents – it makes no difference,' she says. 'And the other ones – Iranians, Afghans, landing on top of all the Libyans and Syrians ... what would Nazan's projects do for them? Not Arabs, but identical in destinies.... All these significant guys are here, they won't go back....

'It's not just Arabs: I know, others are worse off still.... What Nazan wants may turn out bland: planting some trees, making a movie. Money irrigates.... It's countries, all competing.... Frontiers stop a human crossing, stop humans helping humans.... It's humans against humans....'

It's not a good story. I say that to Jalelah – she's impatient.

'We're good, Jalelah,' I tell her. 'We must cling to that. Our intentions....'

She interrupts, 'You don't enquire, Vadim. That's a weakness. Everybody knows – especially in France – there's finance coming in: religion, services, charities – and politics. The wretched of the earth – stay wretched, but they're mercenaries. All the big states are involved, the little ones.... Building, buying. Bullying. Recruiting, selecting, chivvying, persuading, lying, goading, redeeming and repenting.... It's not just a romance, having fun with an historical identity. Everything we touch, and

Nazan touches – it's live, there is surveillance from all sides.... It's not for us.'

'Forget it,' I say. 'Forget your reservations. Discussion's ended. Let's leave what's too complicated, out of our hands. Concentrate on us. Escaping failure, we've landed in the fire....'

Both of us, we think of fire, most of the time. It's cold. We're frozen through.

*

I could stay with Letty; help pull Silva's load; love Jalelah, who would skitter off, just at the thought. Only Nazan has a substance – Nazan the impregnable, owning every horse in every race, and backs them all to lose. I'm not considered, not by anyone. It's good. It's excellent. That way you don't need spin a tale.

'Don't be involved,' Jalelah says: 'You are involved. Think how to get out.'

'One world, Jalelah,' I say. 'It's a way. My principle. Maybe it's suicide for everyone, but it's a triumph nonetheless....'

'You're poison,' Jalelah shouts. 'Look at the money! Where it comes from. You wanted liberation – what you push towards is not! All the things you hate – money, that is its source and destination. The despots, bigotry, plots – it's Nazan made enormous.... For us here – we're in the middle of a battle where we are the weakest part – destitute and ignorant....'

'We'll talk our way,' I say. 'Language. Not faith. It's what this place is famous for, although – perhaps it never was quite so – and now, the wretched of the earth.... They're everywhere, they're here. We have a weapon, Jalelah: moral autonomy, remember. It's a shaky deal, but hold to that ... we have no allies, possibly that is a strength....'

'The world's not one,' she shouts again. 'The world's a fleet of rafts, there's cannibals, cadavers, pirates and pilgrim fathers: – reflect, Vadim! Some seas boil and others dry, and when they dry there isn't land laid bare, there's sand, quicksand, and down and down you sink...: we drift, we row without a goal, there is no land what's underneath us as we float around, the cities and their towers – they're forests, waltzing kelp.... We have to find our spot that's not submerged nor waterless....

'Your wilderness is burnt – a bonfire, everybody dancing round and scorched, the mansion torched – Letty's taken screaming off, obsessed with guilt for what she hasn't done, and terrified by what she cannot do....'

'It's always been too late for anything,' I say. 'The destiny is written, in black and bitter ink, our bile – we stand and weep as the decree scrolls out. The dispossessed....'

'Won't get it back, what they have lost,' she says. 'It wasn't great. It's gone. We never had it, so we never lost. Moral autonomy – it never flew! What's new? Survival. Bring back animals. Let's study them – it's true, the bigger ones eat everything that's weak, dead or alive – that's us, Vadim. We're carrion on the lam. Don't hope to change the species – that is why we came to rule the forest, eat our cubs, and burn our huts and crops in a raptus of despair or with delight in leaping flames, and stripping off and prancing in the fires, and dance and dance, until we drop. *'Et je danse'* – that's what the poet said before he changed his job and trafficked arms and did his dirty deals.... That sounds like me: it isn't me. That time has gone. It never was, when we could scrump the peaches and the curiosities, the pineapples, the Chinese gooseberries.... And you will go to court, Vadim, for what you did or didn't do, and what you didn't stop or tell the cops ... and now they're after you, and – alas – they're after me as well ... and we'll both rot in holding cells and execution yards, mock sentences and mocking executions all our long and tortured lives...!'

'I can't agree the portrait is of me, resembles me in any way,' I say. 'Maybe you're right. Where shall we go? And can we get there anyway? We must support them all, our comrades....'

'As best we can,' says Jalelah.

*

'Do you know why there's suffering?' Jalelah asks.

'No,' I say. 'I know there is. Does it make a difference that I know, and suffer for the suffering?'

'Vicarious suffering? It sounds an easy choice,' she says.

'I thought I knew what it all signified. I read the logic and mathematics, but then they started being modern, even contemporary, and I lost the thread. It seems I'm mostly wrong,' I say.

'You could be more specific,' Jalelah says. 'Name people, bring in your family, the country. How much cash you have, if you have a genuine qualification, if you could go to jail for false documents, for witnessing war crimes, or crimes *tout court*? Exist!'

'We are in France – a country whose people suffer and have caused great suffering to others, for centuries, when they had no business interfering.... We have friends, some Arab, many not – some unemployed, some scraping by, some unrespected, living helter-skelter lives....'

That is the truth she wants – it doesn't signify. I tell her, not knowing where she's getting to.

'You act guilty,' says Jalelah. 'I presume you are. You hide everything you can. I don't feel safe with you. Your friends – are worse, probably they're more determined. They've done everything you are suspected of.'

'That's true for certain, yes,' I say.

'I want to get away from you,' she says. 'You hide from me, you have no strategy of protection, you, me, or others.'

'Of course,' I say. '"France" is a construct, cobbled together from different tribes and wanderers, strangers, reluctant passers-through and clans ... like we all are. We're living in a sieve, a metaphor. The rules, the bosses, change continually. Some take it seriously and try to find the rudder or the reins ... history is the horse, they say, strong, not straight.... It isn't so: the horse is an animal, just like you; history? – it doesn't even breathe, still less jump fences.'

'You must find that what you believe is true, makes life difficult for you,' she says. 'But it helps you avoid the suffering.'

'That is the hope,' I say. 'People expect you to sympathise with suffering. It's maybe not the most important thing. Conclusions – those are interesting. Not death, but all that comes before.'

'I've a conclusion,' says Jalelah. 'Here, we've concluded not a thing. Take note: I'm finishing with you, Vadim....'

And that she does.

All that we do and are – dies. All life – expires. The rest – the perceptions, the things we dream of, think, make strut on to a cloudy stage – it doesn't die, because it doesn't live. We – some of us – aspire to reach immortal mists. They're insubstantial – they roll on, far far above, like methane from the cows we farm.... The cows, the gas – aren't good for us. Too bad....

That is the philosopher's vase – life, death, and air, inside. There's no design on the outside – maybe ... inside? No maker's mark.

It's all there, the question; irresolvable, and resolved. Jalelah is life and death: when she goes, all that's left is immortal – but so what?

'Finish with me, Jalelah,' I say. 'And stay.'

That she does as well.

*

'We must be our children,' I say. 'To evaluate us, our designs, our passions, and our campaigns. They try real hard to love us, even harder than we try to love ourselves, and they bring other people in, and props, landscapes, scenery – and being small and feeling sick. We must indulge, and then ... the children make allowances, but no one's told them they must forgive. I think that's right. They oughtn't.

'If we aren't our children, Jalelah, where do new things take shape?'

'I don't want my children,' says Jalelah. 'Bearing them is tough, being them – is worse. True, there's some I've seen, not available, but quite delicious. I don't want yours either, Vadim. You breed a nest of wriggling things, not someone you can take for walks.'

'Most people have a lot of kids, right now,' I say. 'It means a lot of love. If you don't have them, where'll you find out anything new, what's to come? It seems to make up for what we just went through and all we missed out on. We were present, and impotent, at the end of civilisation, then of the world. We decided not to have progeny. When you decide that, you renounce using part of yourself, like it was an accessory.'

'This is mawkish,' says Jalelah. 'But it shows we were not right, not fit for what we were thought we were.'

'What we were seeing,' I say. 'Witnessing. It showed we hadn't understood.'

We laugh. 'We're terrible witnesses!' says Jalelah. 'Imagine! The cops would think we'd done it, whatever it had been. Some laws say we did.'

'If anything's been changed, fixed,' I say. 'It wasn't us that fixed it. For most things we've a manifesto, but that's it!'

'Enough!' says Jalelah. 'I've had the threats and promises, experienced it all, your fears and mine. There's nothing new. And now – there's rules and laws, we don't know what they are, but they're tight. No one tells what they are, because they don't know; or they know. You won't. What space is left? That space is where the gecko lived, between the floorboards, but you share it with a clutch of *fachos,* deniers of everything except themselves.'

'It's not you,' I say. 'If all that's left is going on the streets, shouting and being clubbed.'

'It's strange,' she says. 'Everyone says we're right, and on the right side – but all the same, they're being clubbed.'

'Too many sinners around,' I say, 'who don't believe in sin.'

We laugh.

Being clubbed, dragged into wagons, is the first intimation of victory. We must applaud, share the cause: turn the tide.

*

'The police,' says Jalelah, 'they say we must go away. Don't ask why, and if we do, they'll put us in a camp and hold us till they have a motivation.'

'Where to?' I ask.

'He said he's not a travel agent,' Jalelah says and laughs. 'He has a turn of wit, for sure.'

'We made a noise, and had no allies. That's disaster, Jalelah,' I say. 'Everybody feels the heat – you can complain. Injustice and stupidity, most people live on that ... if you're new or young, it's best keep schtum.'

'I want to run, then stop,' says Jalelah. 'I know there's people, an immense place, where I can feel at home. You run, and keep on: if you stop, you find you have to run again, or shake to bits ... and there's no people who would welcome you, enjoy you, make you at home. That's the contrast, Vadim, the cultural divide. Your name, your documents – all false. Mine – ineradicable, all true as true.'

'Yes,' I say. 'That means you have the choice. You'll stick where we end up – and I'll escape.'

'In the end,' she says. 'We drink the apples, and eat the cows. They might drink you, Vadim. You're often drunk. Eat me, when I am ripe. Or old. Make me cheese. Or turn me into little cows to fry or dry; and you – a wise trunk, stuck in your wilderness. No roots, but imposing, vertical all the same. Grey and scaly, with an elephant stuck on behind.'

'They'll see us,' I say, 'but they'll think we're something else.'

'I shall be,' she says. 'In the can. A mackerel. On a Saturday. Very circumscribed.'

'I shall play the carillon,' I say. 'Marquis Yi of Zeng had a set of bells: sixty-five. Never exceeded. I shall do my best. We shall improvise.'

The countryside ... running down and shredding. The sea – sucked dry, or dribbling down a vent, putting out the fire, the orange, in the core. 'After'? A heavy word. Riding a clinker.

'Perhaps the countryside involves us in an adjustment we can't make,' she says. 'Then there's the villagers, and their police. They'll spy on us.'

'Not the sea,' I say. 'The river. Live by it, on it. Watch what comes down. There's no exchange – nothing goes up. The locals won't have time to spy. The river's dirty – the Buriganga's swollen, full of crap – you need to find somewhere up high to stay. They add the top two storeys, made of cardboard – sometimes floor nine collapses into eight....'

We laugh. 'The countryside is not a good idea,' says Jalelah: 'It's crowded. That's why the police want us to go there.'

'No, it's politics,' I say. 'We saw it, when Silva and the soldiers came – we thought it was for vanity and fun. They were keeping an eye, that's all. We're subversive characters – all the money that's not ours ... where will it end up?'

'It's right,' she says. 'They must keep an eye.... The town is not a good idea, and we can't stay – it's better than the river bank, is all. Everyone is foreigners now. We're anonymous, but they know us all. I love them, all of them, of us, but you can't trust a soul.'

'It wasn't ours,' I say. 'The money. We were the servants. Or rather – we told the servants what to do. We were the upper servants, above stairs. We welcomed, entertained. You danced, Jalelah, in those days. What did that mean? Only Nazan had a plan, kept it to herself. Probably each morning it was changed.'

'We have to concentrate,' she says. 'Find somewhere we know how to live. I don't want you on my back, Vadim. Let's be clear. I'm an artist, I can't carry too much weight.'

'I know,' I say, 'we resent each other. Hate is good – it clears things out – the pipes, the sentiments: like chlorine. That can win wars!'

'You can't do anything, Vadim. People get angry with you, staring at them, being arrogant,' she says. 'Ridiculous – like a boss, but unemployed.'

I can't respond. So what? I think.

'The countries here,' she says. 'What we call the Evening Lands – they've made up for it – if there were Arabs or guys in India, China, all down there, that once had aspirations – these Lands have settled scores. Times over. Modern weapons and the old – the four horsemen and the new models of the Gatling gun. That is the history for now. And more, much more, to come.'

'Well?' I ask. 'Resist it? Beautify? Change the labels, the motives, call back the soldiers, send them as bankers? Who are we to take a stand? – and how? And why?'

'We're at the start again,' she says. 'Except that now, we can't have trust in one another, you and I.'

*

'What we do, we must do it the American way,' she says. 'On film. The final cut.'

'In the movie,' I ask. 'What impressed you most?'

'Certainly it was the cow. Winched up in the sky for barbecuing,' she says.

'I thought it was a buffalo,' I say. 'The water kind. You're drifting, Jalelah. I'm not American. That's a mistaken category. Putting people in a crowd like that, because they're all the same. It's virtually an insult. Describing you, because you live somewhere, in a place, have documents.

'What everybody wants is what the Americans wanted and can't have. So, it went on film. There, you can want to win or lose. Say it different, make a different movie.

'It's finished, Jalelah: making a story. The best ones have been made, now there is singing. Everybody sings along, it's quite infectious. Dancers? They always seem so vulnerable. Concentrated and on the edge of balance. Just a jostle, and it's done.... Down into the pit they go.'

'There's always movies, Vadim,' says Jalelah. 'But you're right. We've had everything in them, over and over. Birth to apocalypse – what's left? Of course, Vadim – *we're* left! We're hungry now: our choice – like everyone will be....'

'No, no,' I say. 'Nothing's discounted. Ways round that, the hunger, will be found. We should set to, get serious, make machines, or track an enzyme – but we can't. We've not been taught. It isn't us. You'd need the capital. Besides – for us, the way we are, it's futile. That's where your moral autonomy gets you – up the creek!'

*

There's a pause, but nothing stops.

Jalelah gestures at me. She wears a half-mask, over her eyes and nose. She gesticulates some more, like a monkey. 'I'm in a troupe,' she says. 'You won't have heard. They teach you circus routines – a little magic, disappearing, being pierced with swords. Tumbling, of course.

'The guy I sleep with – he's on split-screens for hours. Riven! Has info on everyone.'

'I'm not near that,' I say. 'I just get troubled, that my analysis might be wrong, cause harm, defeat my own side – though I know, it's all conditional and shifting. You can be right in principle, but little massacres take place, you're never questioned, but there is responsibility ... at least somewhere ... it's been noted down. Impossible to verify, of course – what's been said and done, all over, every evening, while you watch the screen, and tell your lie, or weep.'

'Exactly,' says Jalelah. 'We don't think like you. We *do*. We're in it, we act, we take the consequences, we're not the watchers in the watchtower, the messengers, the carrion-pickers ... we take a side, and suffer for it. The language of our hands and bodies, set into signs, scant ideograms – connects us, and links us to the cause. Where you have nothing but your raggedy clothes and scarecrow spread of arms in useless threats – we take the rap!'

'I envy you,' I say, 'Except....'

'You can't slough off uncertainty, your inner strifes, what you think, don't know, and can't work out. You have to risk and suffer, Vadim,' she says, earnestly, faking it. 'Otherwise – you're dross. A sediment.'

'I see you're soldiers, Jalelah,' I say. 'But you're unarmed. Childrens' crusades – they all end bad. You can't be bought, but can be sold. You'll end up on the slab – the morgue, or as fresh flounders at the fishmongers....'

'If you're armed,' she says. 'You risk real fights, real armies. We keep a long arm's length from that. We're not enrolled, not under contract. There's synchrony, not sympathy, between us and our side – the other warriors. We take the rap, for sure – but where we do it, mostly we end up in jail, not in the grave.'

'I'm only part convinced....' I say. She interrupts –

'There isn't time for that,' she says. 'Convincing you won't change a thing. The process of conversion takes for ever, one by one, and needing cash, philosophers, all that. Too late! We don't convince – we show. We do. Enough that *we*'re convinced: why wait for you? Join me, if you can, and will. If not – you're undergrowth, just seashore pebbles, shifting with the tides ... a little here a fraction there ... passivity in simulated action, that is you....'

'Individuals looking for a new form of organisation....' I say. 'That's you. It's not enough. Russia had Lenin and the Bolsheviks, the war, the peasants, 1905, the Tsar and the

Tsarina.... And then it was a close, exhausting struggle that ended bad, and cost....

'You have a platoon of Kerenskys, and think you have a cure, Jalelah: you play at rasputing.'

'It ended, Vadim,' Jalelah says. 'Revolution. Always ends. You said it. It must not. Whatever it turns out to be.'

'I'm mechanical,' I say. 'Maybe what you want won't end. What *I* want, always will. But – people eat while mine is going on. Your people starve. That's the difference – but, you're probably right. I can't change, and I'm an obstacle.'

'You're a butcher too,' she says. 'When it suits.'

'What they say about the mind reflecting the real world,' I say. 'I believe it, but it puzzles me. Maybe I'm an obscurantist too! Just think. Mind must be part of what it must reflect. It seems it is a mirror in a frame, a glass, silvered, inert. But if there is a will – to play the part assigned by destiny? Or is it by necessity? It's simple, but it puzzles me....'

'I can't argue with you, Vadim,' says Jalelah. 'It makes me and mine sound like mercenaries.

'One-track professionals.... Machines with orders and a stipend.'

*

> '... language is always a little ahead of thought and a little more impetuous than love.... The imagination must take too much for thought to have enough. The will must imagine too much in order to realize enough.'
>
> Gaston Bachelard, *Air and Dreams*

I may not see Jalelah again. If we meet – we could be on opposing sides. I'm more materialist than she – but she has mates, comrades, they share ... There's food, excess of games and justifications too.

I must go back to where I know there is a fridge.

*

'Go away, Vadim,' says Nazan. 'You're tainted, compromised. What happened to the Arabs? Kurds too. You were supposed ... explaining.... Faith and destiny – and suffering. All for a spat with Jalelah, that neither understood. I'll bet some genitals were put on to the scale.

'Silva is different – she's a real mercenary, not a sponger. She has a contract. There's an agreement. She depends on me. I clean her soul.

'You're in dispute. Who do you belong to? What are your obligations? Do you have rights? Which ones? You've none from me – I don't hand them out. You bring them with you, or you'll not be given them by me.'

Letty stands beside her, wrinkling her face: a little flapping of the hands ... she's complicit, of course – apologetic too. Her flesh is weak, the spirit maybe even more....

'I did the rounds, Nazan,' I say. 'Tried to be good, then tried obedience, then a cover-up, and after all had failed, to make a stand on principle. No doubts, and no retreats, just recognition of necessity. And in the end, it all came clear. I realised – necessity lives here, Nazan, it's crept in bed with you....'

'You have to see where movement stirs,' she says. 'The ladies and the gentlemen – they haven't understood; there's little soldiers everywhere, in uniform and not. We all need cash to live – there's lots who don't have cash, and they don't live. My plan ... the wretched of the earth ... a wretchedness that spreads ... if not peace, then something else ... if not survival, then....'

She holds back, won't set out the plan.

'It's set up as a charity,' says Silva. 'Not like those condescending, frantic, bureaucratic ones. Gawping at the starving poor, a nickel for their impotence and fecklessness ... their isolation and their hopeless state. Emergencies? – behold! a hit and run of bags of flour. Nazan's support is calm, gentle, and it lasts. It's not a state, nor superstate, engaged in last-ditch rescuing, life-saving ... coaxing the tender-hearted to part with some small change ... saving a martyred people briefly in the news. The little ones especially, the innocents – they tweak the rich ... no fault's assigned ... no condemnation of the banks, the landlords, the seed contractors, the bombers, the corrupt ... just acts of gods inhuman, just happenings unjust. Pay up, and keep them quiet....'

'Nazan has in mind – to save communities,' Letty says. 'Understanding the bad that happens in the lives of striving, unassuming people.'

'It's much much more,' says Silva. 'The Brits set up exams and competitions, recruiting Gurkhas. Soldiers for an empire not their own, turned into an elite of mercenaries. Like circus tigers. Pensioned off quite mean. We'd work to find defenders ... undefeated....'

'Recruiting. Nazan's always worked that way: recruiting,' I say. 'She wants an army, in waiting, ready to go: no criterion of faith or nationality, but ... everybody knows, she requires complete loyalty to her idea.... The troops must have a lifetime's motivation.

'Men – have no constancy. Women, they have more rage, but everyone who's selected, nurtured and sustained – they are enrolled for life. Resistance: justice: mutual aid. Tradition, with novelty....'

'No parties, no despots, no gurus: no movements scattering like dust,' says Nazan, sounding irritated. 'I have to think it through, to make it solid ... stop being threatened or bought off....'

'No religion, no new states, no generals,' Letty chants.

'More secret armies, more armed groups,' I say. 'It sounds an old, old fantasy – that all will turn out for the best, if good traditionalists play their part and take the lead.... Elites of bodyguards, taking their orders from chiefs invisible, anonymous.'

'You see spies and cartels everywhere,' says Silva. 'When my group came, we had some harmless rituals. All that is past – a spectacle, no more....'

'It's not for me,' I say. 'I wouldn't qualify, and wouldn't join.'

'Then,' Nazan says. 'Starve in the dark. Your scepticism has led you nowhere ... or better, has led you back to me.... For you, see it or don't – I am survival. You're an extreme, a failing specimen. What we need now – is groups of guys who have at heart the future of a species reinforced and independent.... These will survive, not plot to kill each other, or compete in building superbombs or ruining their trade. As for the rest – it's got too late, my dears... Alas – I can't save everyone ... no one can....'

'It's gone like disco,' Silva says. 'Trying to keep up. Is this the end, beautiful friend? That's what they ask. Are you connected to the scene? What a laugh...! And you, Vadim! Your new age riffs evoke passivity and lingering on trivia, a candy floss of bliss and gloss.... It's you, and it is out of place and time....'

*

'Dump your pack here,' Caleb says, pointing to a blind arch. 'Welcome. I hope you're not a Russian.... We're here to flag up our Sufi tendency – it isn't popular with everyone....'

'I'm here for charity,' I say. 'Like you. I'm escaping one, but I need yours. I know you Sufis don't just spin.'

'We gave R and R to all the caravans,' he says. 'Sent them on their way, with new cultures and ideas tucked in between the camels' humps.'

'I could have carried charity to dodgy places, Caleb,' I tell him. 'I didn't think that it would work – turned into its opposite, traduced by spies and cops ... I could have tried – but I don't trust my friends and enemies....'

'Welcome anyway,' he says. 'If you're hot property, tomorrow you move on. Just leave your name....'

'My name is Russian, but I'm stateless, Caleb,' I say. Anxiety and dread suffuse me. 'This document won't tell my tale.... I'll dump my name together with my pack.'

And so I do.

'We don't want your name,' he says. 'We'd exchange things, not symbols. If you bring more symbols, chat about metaphor, about how this is really that, and poetics this, and space is that.... I'll close you out. Enough! We want concreteness. Look at this caravanserai – it's huge! When I go, tomorrow, possibly – it's yours. You stay. You can't just take my charity and leave....'

'No, no,' I say. 'That's not my plan. This is just bricks – there's no one here, no animals, just nothing – straw and rags....'

'It's history, my friend,' says Caleb. 'Faith. Inspiration. It can all be yours.'

'I don't want it,' I say, much alarmed. 'There's many many things that I don't want – and this is one that will not move, is not an idea that changes as you look, not an image sufficient in itself – just a set of boxes, cylinders, made of mud brick, where winds go tangoing that don't exist outside....'

'Enough!' he says. 'This was a test. You failed. If you want charity, you have to stay – not wander off, looking for a better place.'

'You're right,' I say. 'All I have is eyes and feet, and a perspective that tells if something's near or far. It's all potential. All mindless stuff.'

'Alas,' says Caleb. 'You really are what I had feared – a robot!'

We laugh.

'This place,' I say, 'is a monument. A granary.'

'I built it,' says Caleb, 'as a memory of the Project. My memory – before the waters rose and swept us all away – was of the industrious; a New York of bats and rats – the scavengers, night crawlers, collectors and collected – the ethnographic cabinet of curiosities.... To me, those terra cotta mounds where we all lived – were empty. For no reason did we need others, company. People were a brute necessity. I feared the neighbours. I – we all – studied, lived so we could identify our God. We were all Sufis – after Sufism, but Sufis too, *avant la lettre.*'

'That's what al-Ghazali says,' I say. 'Studying reality, the material, the knowledge dealing with the tangible, the measurable, the reasonable – brings sadness, disenchantment. Meditating on the intangible, the imaginary – brings happiness.'

'Ah yes,' says Caleb. 'But – why do we want that, happiness? What is it for? What, if anything, do we do with it? The contemplation of air, of space? What futility! Hide and seek – with God the vain ... playing at *cache-cache* ... maybe he has furuncles. Is that the revelation?'

'You'd leave me this?' I ask. 'A granary without a grain? The memory – is yours: these flattened domes, the tiny *fessure* way up high – to let the creatures in and out, unseen by us, down here – you'd let this go?

'Your history? That's not what I want – there's no one comes, no food, no bed....'

'You don't need anything of that,' says Caleb. 'You're not near death, and not a saint. Those get charity – you don't. You've nothing, so you can't give charity. Not even revelation. I give you this huge structure: fill it as you will. Make something of my memory ... and if you've nothing you can give, no concept, no activity to fill it, even just adorn a corner where you dropped your bag of rags ... well! If you've nothing, nothing to trade, exchange ... can't play a flute, or dance, or tell a tale, or whistle through your teeth ... eat and sleep: that's what you want, and what you have to give. It's pitiful.'

'All the same, Caleb,' I say, 'I feel you're giving up, and moving out. Me, I'm an optimist.

'And yet, the people who don't see us, what my ex-boss calls the wretched – would they be proud of us, you and I?'

'I've nothing to be ashamed of,' Caleb says. 'There's this huge structure, all my creation: empty, so if it floods or burns, if it's bombed, explodes – no one can get hurt. My Project, Vadim. Now – let's hear your Plan!'

We laugh. 'There's nothing shameful in reflecting,' I say. 'It's like the mind, the mirror. An automaton.'

'Everyone has worth,' says Caleb. 'Waiting for someone to set a price on us – it is the game. The longer you wait, are patient, the better it will be for you.'

'Are you sure this is a granary, Caleb?' I ask. 'The dark is good – but you need pits or silos – dry and quiet to stop the little seeds waking up to sprout.'

‘Hmmm,’ he says. ‘That sounds quite plausible. I thought up this monster, attributed its purpose, off the cuff. I’ve never seen one functioning.... Help me to rectify, my friend....’

And that we do.

‘Listen!’ he says. ‘That tinkling. My Monk arrangements.’

It’s like a wire flapping on a brick. ‘That’s almost zero, Caleb,’ I say. ‘And – in the context, how do you live here? There’s been the bombs, the futurists, the throwbacks ... progressives, fundamentalists ... no caravans for years ... the drought, resettlements.... Is there still room for Monk?’

He doesn’t answer. When it’s light, I leave: the discussions are too fleeting, there’s no sense, no answers work, nor are required. Caleb’s a good guy. He gives where he should take. The empty granary, its smooth and graceful corners, low domes, nearly flat, like on cisterns, blends with the universe as though they both won’t one day collapse in dust – walk a bit away, and you can’t see it sticking up out from the plain, like it did last evening when I had arrived. Sufi architecture – so discreet, you can pack in towers and esplanades on a corner lot, make a city on the edge of an escarpment and it hovers there and doesn’t tumble – and Sufi builders, poised and rustling, always coming in a ten percent under the estimate and a week before the deadline.... That’s why they’re distrusted, hard to find: forever undercharging....

It’s strange – the absence of a building, any one; or of anyone – it should reassure me there’s no danger imminent. Instead – I hurry on. Quite spooked. Any clustering of people and of things will bring relief.

*

The town is short of things to sell. People – I’m sure they have no cash – wander up and down, looking at worn-out stuff, fingering the rolls of cork and cracked linoleum, the sacks of crumbling caramels ... unsellable, unbuyable. I see Caleb: my spirits make a hop, as if he's an old old friend.

'There's lots I didn't explain to you,' he says: 'Interesting things, ideas I've had. There's people here, who paid not to be taken off as soldiers: reverse mercenaries, you would say. Their money's gone in avoiding drama; to have another ordinary day, drab and undemanding: paying to be left alone, another day before you end up on the butcher's stall, like a rabbit with the paws cut off, the head drooping, dripping in a little plastic bag.'

'I'm interested in such things,' I say. 'I may have misjudged people living under stress, necessity ... it's like a maddening breeze....'

'You say that as if you know you've made mistakes,' he says. 'I'm not sure you're one who admits to things.

'The people here are mixed, they rub along, they don't take part in fights ... it's a mistake. You keep on being occupied – bombed from the air as well. You seem to be strategic – or to have an aura. Something special. Like a shield. It's best to have an interest, fight for it, wait for reprisals, then....

'The day before is drab: the day after – dull and grey.'

'Tell me,' I say, 'The granary. You'd never fill it – it's immense. Did you find it, build it – or make the adjustments that make it ... well ... resemble itself? What it's supposed to be? Almost, it could be just what you say ... empty....'

'Find, or build?' he asks, and fixes me – manages a twinkling smile: 'It's really the same thing – if you're a builder, like myself.'

'You need be very strong,' I say, quite overwhelmed, 'to keep things standing, then, when they're knocked down, to leave the ruins far behind, go round and round the world with nothing but your little telephone.'

'Rabbits,' he says. 'Rabbit Island. Coney Island. Dead or alive, my home.'

'You are a turncoat, Caleb, a traitor. A convert. You're right,' I say. 'I feel for you, it's a line I cross and re-cross. No one knows our heads: it's like the granary was heaped to the top with my desires – a huge tumescence, full and ready.... Then ... we leave. We run away.'

'That was before,' he says. 'When we had history that went on and on, always different, but the shapes were always the same, and few, like an infant's toy ... despots and reform, drought, fire, extinction – discovery and settlement, genocide and crucifixions. Now ... it all comes on at once.... Stay or leave – here, you don't exist.'

'You have the granary,' I say. 'Though upkeep must be tough.... Even if it falls down, you have to pay: the sprawl is more expansive, the concession more expensive.'

'It's a fraud,' he says. 'The fiscal table. Look under "bath-hall", "domed basilica", for the rates.... It was constructed to be empty. Taxing emptiness is ridiculous. People say it was to house the dead. They make more noise, they're numbered, remembered, more than the living are. They know more than us – they had an expiry date. We don't know! Unimaginable – such an important day....

'I see it filled with noise. Chatter. Life stories. Complete – down to the last unexpected trivial detail, totally predictable. There's the tables, where you can verify each happenstance. Such subversion – the tales of disappointment, the bullying, mishandling! What a noise, what a racket! The building could have been ten times bigger, to hold it all – unfairness – disproportion.... Mockery. The angry litany of people disappeared. The lesson?

'Don't join anything, don't pay anyone, resist the *pizzo*; join in the prayers, pay someone to do your military service, even if it's twenty-five years – it's a man's life, a woman's too.

'A building like that, where the living honour the dead, wish to be like them in their wisdom, knowing the last things – it looks empty, sure....'

He pauses. We take a glass of tea – it's poured, a golden stream from a great height, spurtles with a rocket's take-off sound: what a relief: micturation – we laugh delightedly.

'I'll tell you why,' I say. 'It looks empty: because there's nothing to put in.'

'Don't say it,' he says. 'A civil place pays other people to do the soldiering, the dying, in their stead. When they can't, the problem is humanity itself. It creeps in, falls all over you, arms and legs, you have to take your bundle, run – some things you cannot pay for, though that's an anomaly, because the essential is what a payment's most essentially for. You can't pay for the most important things – avoiding them, saying you did when for sure you didn't do. A Mass, a tomb of porphyry, the most wonderful you can imagine – you only pay for those too late. After; after everything – see my wink, my nod! What comes after....'

'I know all that, Caleb,' I tell him. 'Everybody does.'

'I never said it was the revelation, naturally,' he says.

*

'You could run a book, or a line of credit. Charge what you like,' I say, leading him on: 'Any sum and any odds, a payment to avoid what's going to happen. To avoid, too, what has happened.'

'That's what we did,' he said. 'Everybody here paid everything they had and now – see how poor they are.'

It's so. There's a long line, silent, waiting for gas.

'Go away,' says the baker: 'I've shut down the oven, come back another day.'

I'm hungry. There's something I love to see, though – the budgerigar, that picks a card. You bet against him. He's a crafty one!

*

'Well,' says Nazan, 'you went there. You saw: it was time someone helped the Arabs. They've had a rotten deal recently, and I was right to lend a hand. Now it's shifting – further South. Some will be Arabs still, then there's the language, and the faith, of course. That is hanging on, but it's like a kettle sprung a leak! Hot everywhere, and fumes, and streams of people, lots of cops.... I used to send out cash, but now it's food they need, but then – I get my food from them, so life gets unpredictable.'

She laughs, and I laugh too, so pleased to be in work again, back with mates, and having met the most *sympa* of guys – Caleb and his monument.

'It's desolate down there,' I say. 'I would have stayed – Caleb knows his music, polystylism still has some traction, and the Sufism he brought over from the States is wild!... Nothing of that's too popular, but he has real estate, there's people ready from elsewhere who will buy him out....'

I ramble on, remember finally to say: 'And Nazan, thank you for the fare....'

Later, Silva says, 'Nazan's militias?... It's a crowded field. People need cash, but don't want to obey. It's hard to trust her, it seems she offers not a principle, but a distant subsidy that might just disappear in smoke.... She needs some generals, but as you know – all twenty field-marshals is her, and every simple soldier too.'

'Be careful,' Letty says. 'What you wish for. Americans set up a militia, it ended up as the state, and threw them out. We need order without slaughter.... Armies and states – they're death with a hundred scythes. They don't protect, defend: people run from them if they can, if they survive. Then – still others are forced to run, the panic grows, there's chaos, massacre.... Regimes are imposed, they kill, and people run.... They run anyway: from fire and water, drought and storm.... All Nazan wants is ... order. That's what people want, until it blows away ... then they look for nature and its state, but no! It's flattened, savannah.... She says – "survive where you are, stay put; away with despots everywhere.... Think liberation, meantime make where you are seem liveable. Some of you will get paid for that...."'

'It's fun to hear enthusiasm,' I say.

*

You don't run for ever. You stop, because you've found a place with nothing and there's nowhere else, or because something's stopped you.

'Is this how ideas make you great and everybody changes because of you?' I ask Silva. 'It's so simple, I didn't know.'

'Of course,' she says. 'That's all you need. There's lots of simple things, simple ideas – all different. All incompatible.'

'I hadn't remembered, Silva,' I say. 'How you are superficial.'

'If you're not all surface,' she says. 'Your insides fall out. You're gloop. Sticky stuff you find on leaves. You told me this before – you don't listen to what you say. I'm a roach – every bit of me's designed to function right.'

'I'm not happy with this,' I say. 'With what I find here. The crew, the analysis. The sponsors.'

'You don't matter, Vadim,' she says. 'You went away and never came back.'

'There's no answer to anything here,' I say. 'It's true, I'm pleased to know I'm right about that. The goal is not to find solutions to stuff, it's how to get together to find what that stuff is ... and it's what everybody knows.'

'Travel's broadened your mind, Vadim,' says Silva. 'It's as broad as the Gobi.'

*

'Somebody knockin' on my door ...'

Getting away. Imperative.

'It's all different here,' Letty says: 'We all have new partners. You're the joker – we forgot to take you out the pack when we began to play.

'It gets harder to keep up, catch up, that's all. We speed up. We have less time for thought.'

'I get modern things backwards,' I say. 'I'm always on the fogey side, because I don't recognise it.'

That knocking – it means someone else wants to use the room. Your time is up, you didn't know it had begun. Being in a room alone means no one can be found to share it; or you. They'll say,

'Here comes another loner, coming in to garden weed or try peyote, write about it.'

*

Kurds. They'd been left out – an unpardonable slip. The brain's cogs wearing down.

*

'I'll teach you aims and holds,' says Silva. 'Types of tree and kinds of wind. Pegging tents and pegging out. A mnemonic for your number, when you're caught; your pay grade when you're ransomed. That's everything you need to know.'

We laugh, I embrace her. Her body yields like taffy. And I'm off, farewell Silva, farewell security.

Letty says she accepts herself, no longer wants self-improvement, nor feels she could do better if she tried.

'That's bad news,' I say. 'Giving up, accepting your defects, not caring ...'

We don't embrace – the strong sensual charge between us still exists. We don't insist.

'I fear for Silva,' says Nazan. 'She's vulnerable – besides, we don't need security here, we need it over there....' and she gestures. 'The more I've contacts here – the more we're threatened there....'

'You suffer less than anyone, Nazan,' I say. 'Even if you lose everything you've staked.'

'Of course you must object to me,' she says. 'Remember: the rich and powerful help the strong. I'm rich and powerful, Vadim, and I stand with them. The rich, they're there to pay the locals – the strong, the educated. Those guys enforce their order on the rest. If things go bad, the powerful everywhere – they run away, surrender; sometimes do heroics. The others play at victims: too bad for them.

'My idea is good – keeping order, having people stay where they are set, and work things out. In practice, we know exactly what it will entail, my dear. Order means force.

'As for you, Vadim, like it or not – you are with the rich and strong. Change sides, and you won't change a thing. You're servile, Vadim. You reflect what is. You come to me for comfort, purpose, and support. I don't trust you, but I must.

'If it's not you – another mercenary will show, and enter for ever in my crew....

'Wherever you end up, everybody knows, you're from a rich and powerful place. If you've cash, they'll envy you, if not – you'll be despised. Make the best of that you can, Vadim.... And, since you can't lead – consider sainthood....' And she laughs.

'I find it sad,' I say. 'If that's survival; survival of the fit....'

'You find it sad,' she says. 'I'll get over it. Your version of the story would be tender: the tales are different for every audience – remember that.'

*

Caleb's gone. The granary's not there, not even left a mound. There might be something underground, I guess, but I don't want to dig.

To see how everything is working out, I have to leave the big trade routes, the cities, civil and uncivil wars, the drought, the punishments, invasions and dependencies. Go further on, into the big trade routes, the cities, and the rest.

I'm volunteer and mercenary. As Nazan says, the foreigner's exaction, the universal tax – lifts all it wants. The white gaze, the coloniser's wink.

'I'm bomber and fanatic, thief and teacher,' I say aloud. 'I come as saviour now....'

It's false. No one wants saving – nature has created millions ... so that some will survive the bombs, the sickness, and the roasting.

The rest is charity.

*

'Welcome to this poor country,' Elise shouts. 'If you're writing a report – we'll give you all the dirt. You won't need to leave your room, and you'll be out of danger.'

'I'm not sure,' I say, 'I need shelter, clearly. But usually I need to get away.'

'Yusef will bike you,' Elise says. 'We had a camel but we swapped it for some sunflowers.'

'They're splendid,' I say. 'And you can tell the time with them.'

'You'll have to draw it,' Elise says, quite brusque. 'How to tell the time.'

She's precise and clear. Yusef, when he shows, is perplexed. He always is.

I didn't realise, Elise disliked me from the first. She wants the rent: – but her small house, or hut, is far from everywhere.

I talk too freely, mention Nazan – 'The Americans,' says Elise. 'In Nicaragua – Reagan set up an army to fight the militias. It went on for years – I hope she knows.'

'What's happening here?' I ask.

'There's gangs and soldiers,' Elise says. 'We revolutionaries – we need a counter-weight.'

'Yusef – where is he?' I ask.

'He's an ethnographer – he says. He's in the lean-to, listening to *mbalax*. He feels he's in exile here – his radio takes the music when the roof is fronds, not tin....' She flaps her hands, exasperated.

I'm silent. Listen with great care and we can hear a rhythm bouncing out, over the savannah – Yusef will be taking notes. The horsemen – maybe they too can hear....

'We rented out the camel,' says Elise. 'It lived here, and it ate too much.'

'No promises,' I say. 'There's people I know who might assist....'

'No, no,' she says. 'No help, no joining things, no charity. No flashy fluent chiefs, rich, with a programme – envied and despised. And here, there's you to be explained. We're bad off as it is. I'd sooner buy a speedball from the guy who comes round here than be dependent on flush guys from who knows where....'

'That's what I think,' I say.

I stay with them, although it's far from anywhere: I know how things are, anyway. Moral autonomy – it's not discussed. We're crowded here. The map says there's many houses –

'The map's a map, it has its voice, relatively it's right, for sure,' she says. 'Time let it down, like it does to all of us. The people – they mostly went away, there's nothing here. We thought if we could stay we'd use, inherit, all there was. It wasn't so.'

'Go or stay, there's no good choice,' says Yusef.

'You're a scholar, Yusef – there's better ways to be connected. You can't get far with radio waves from Senegal....' I say.

'Oh no,' he says. 'The distance is enormous, but I tune in, and I am there. At least – I am not here. If I connect real bright and loud – I'm here; the music comes in to the house. I want to be, live, exist – over there, where the music's played, far far away, and I can follow it, invention, inspiration that is hard for me to bear, stuck here on my own, and one day perhaps I'll not come back....'

When I'm not talking to Elise, hearing what she might have been and might still be and probably won't want, consoling Yusef, with the *mbalax* on the radio, constantly, like for a bet, a record-break, those '30s American marathons of dance to see who could still stagger on after weeks of fox-trot and slow waltz.... I walk about the village, its deserted clumps and slender mounds ... and think them, Elise and Yusef, dead. Killing each other; or by chance, or fanatics ... and wonder why it's them who die and not myself, being here and asking for it, though the guilt, depression, dread and fear that go with terror, the fear of death by strangers' hands, has not yet materialised, not been uncovered yet....

Is this all created by the foreigner's gaze? All that I see? The black translated into white, like a printed negative? And yet – I'm not real white, and Elise and Yusef are quite vehement they are not black, not Senegalese, though blacks transport Yusef away from what he hates, what makes him sick.... To him, the Senegalese are nonetheless quite primitive, though *mbalax* is as crossed-over, polystyled, as any pair of dancing legs can be.

'We decided,' says Elise, 'so we must stick it out, and risk. We're visible, and tempting. We must be neutral, not declare, not stand for anything except just standing here, displaying nothing but reluctant presence. Just being. Leave us be.'

'We stick it out,' says Yusef, holding back a laugh. 'We're dry old sticks. But, Vadim – you *do* stick out. We're revolutionaries, of course – but you're a Red. You attract attention, because you're anomalous. A colour not found in paint-boxes now: like goose-green, gold leaf or lapis lazuli....'

'We don't want help,' says Elise: 'We want our camel back. And everything to change.'

I think of Jalelah. ‘You could dance, Elise,’ I say. ‘There’d be a vacancy – I know a dancer who’s turned on to militancy.... Open a school – a conservatoire, salons – gala nights....’

‘Don’t strive, Vadim,’ she says. ‘Dancing to the radio? It isn’t what I want ... it wouldn’t leave a mark, or trace a path.’

‘Don’t add to our distress, Vadim,’ says Yusef. ‘You’ll make things worse. When things get desperate, we’ll stand in line with all the rest. Those defending us – they attract vendetta, and threats....’

‘You’re poison,’ Elise says. ‘You and your boss. Things as they might be – you can’t deliver, and you come to us and make disaster. Go away. Make your enquiries somewhere else.’

And that I do.

*

‘...injustice lurks in the pursuit of justice for all...’

Judith N. Shklar

‘Law?’ I hear Nazan shout. ‘I never mentioned law. It’s absent or it’s twisted where there’s chaos, or there’s despots. No one cares about it there, not either way. The context, Vadim! The situation. You didn’t properly ask. I never spoke of justice – self-defence was all my theme. I offered direction where there’s none. You didn’t offer anything ...’

‘I didn’t feel I knew ... or that I ought,’ I say. ‘It was the camel dominating – the absent beast, the lasting love.’

‘Catastrophe by error, or by regime, with law or with wild panic; running, falling down and being trampled,’ Nazan explains. ‘In any case, those all need explanation ... a means to see what’s caused by malice, and what by intent: pursuit of someone else’s goals that sets your hut on fire. Then you can start to turn it round – redressing, fighting back....'

'The life-world's changed for ever, Nazan. My pair – whether by humans or by science, nature ... they knew that nothing could redress, set up the twisted fire-scarred timbers, restore a continuity....' I say.

'Whatever your analysis,' Nazan says, breathing threateningly down the 'phone, 'you showed them nothing. You left them ignorant. That's unforgivable. If there's no cure, when you can make a diagnosis, it's a first step....'

'They thought the first step went straight to the abyss,' I say.

'They knew what they wanted....'

'Oh Vadim,' Nazan says. 'One want leads on to many more. It's all connected up.'

'I can't be sure,' I say. 'It doesn't feel that anything is linked up right, cause and effect are crazy clowns, the universe careens. And if it's all connected, you can't do anything without re-ordering the everything. That's all that is: you can't change one tessera without the dome falls down. And if you have a skeleton key to all the world – it skips away, it falls into a black hole ... or in a rats' nest, where it lies glistening and out of reach, like that city on a hill, where everyone's an executioner. Let's say – it's like a country made of wool. Pull a loose end and – either it unravels, or it makes a knot, immense and dense. There is no other outcome. That's radical change for sure: – to clumping, or to primal state.

'What starts the pulling of the thread – is quite irrelevant. It could be popes or donkeys, winch or algorithm – what matters, is that once it starts, it can't be stopped, its progress cannot be foreseen, whether it ends in "start again", or Armageddon. Besides, for me, they're much the same....'

'There is your truth, at last, poor dear,' Nazan says. 'You can't stand one brick upon another brick – so that explains your love of chaos. And from chaos come the executioners. You know I'm right!

'Your friend Caleb, though – he could build. An empty granary! What magnificence!'

'Caleb – a musician, above all. Before everything,' I say. 'Like Jalelah before she sought anonymity in the mass: – she danced.'

'Pouf!' says Nazan. 'Am I not a revolutionary? Your models, Elise, Yusef – forever hopeful, forever disappointed, waiting for the great change.... Which great change? Directory, consulate, terror, empire, war, monarchy, republic, empire, republic, war, terror, empire, war, terror, Nepmen, famine, Plans and terror, war and terror ... retreat, reform, collapse, deportations, occupation ... which trajectory, which part, do I belong to? It should be easy to fit in somewhere; take the tiller, give the wheel some turns? And where are you, Vadim?

'You see the revolution open the cage door. The limp canary blinks, stands on the threshold ... chirp, chirp, it says. "I have a song – just let me catch my strength. Can that cage door be closed again?"'

'Maybe the canary dies,' I say, irritated. 'The empty open cage – a message ... in an esperanto that everybody understands and no one speaks.'

'Carry on,' says Nazan. 'So long as the money – my money – lasts. Then look out for yourself, Vadim.'

*

'What am I looking for that no one is ignorant of?' I ask myself.

'It's clumsy, it's the case.'

Nazan says, 'You're transparent, like a leaf. Thin, just ribs and main stem, no green or brown, closed in a book for years. The leaf's not interesting – the book – perhaps.... "Where you go, people know exactly about themselves, and what is over their heads. Not ideas and thoughts – but cops and money-lenders. What's left for you to do? They all have other beliefs and principles to yours – your uncertainties ... and you've no state behind you. You're closer to this state, that one, to this strategy, that future ... maybe it'll all be quite new, to you, to everyone."'

I can't talk to Silva: she has her special drama, and a real paradise, not one concocted by humans – but the rounded green hills and vales of Armenia....

Letty is naive, and I'm more naive than her.

Jalelah – she was the best and brightest. Not a trace.... And Nazan was right. People you meet know more about themselves than you ever will.

Silva said, 'Your head is full, Vadim. No point in trying to pour more in. What you most need – is cash. You're a born mercenary. Someone else will take the burdens you can't lift, and – you'll even be paid for being well accoutred. Spy, publicist, reporter, anecdotalist, philosopher. You're made for all of these, because they're all the same. All you lack – is ambition. Passivity's an advantage, though. You could try to be elected as a something: maybe the life will spur you on.... You won't want to leave it, the attention; being taken seriously, whatever you think to say. With your reluctant pose – you could reach the top. Don't send me to fight a war, though – I'm not taken in....'

'Cheap and flimsy, Silva,' I told her. 'Your ranting. Not what I am, but what I can do. To you.'

'I'm the movie,' Silva said. 'When I die, I'm sent to space. My mates are there already. I'll twinkle: not at you. And if in combat I've been cut in two, I'll be the heavenly twins!'

We leave it there. Soldiers – so solemn!

*

Letty told me – Nazan takes money from the rich, the would-be despots: reformers, intriguers, men of faith and hope.... And she uses it for purposes quite other: – far from the faith and hope.

'It's dangerous,' Letty said. 'You never know. If they find out you've used their cash to plot against them....'

'Nazan knows about keeping distances,' I say. 'Just think – what is not a gamble? Money spent is money gone, gone for ever, with its own legs and wings. Its own colours. Its own campaigns.'

'It's not like that at all. That's you talking, Vadim,' Letty says. 'These guys, however much they want and have – they're possessive about how it's spent and where it's gone.'

'I'm sure it's spread around,' I said. 'It's hard to pin down an expenditure, and trace a blame back to an origin; especially when the origins are hope and faith. Nazan does not believe: not at all in either, not faith nor hope.... Possibly, a little more than zero she believes in hope. But – belief is something she can't believe in.'

Maybe she's faster, riskier, than I could have thought. She won't tell, won't share – it's good, everyone but her stays clean and ignorant.

It's all new; I know nothing about what's new. Running away was new – once more. Staying, resisting – it's a gamble. Usually it hasn't worked, but those who tried it – they're all dead. Mostly, everyone who tries the new – is dead. Like those who lived the old. For most, when they are threatened, how they react makes no difference at all. Other forces take the stage....

Who is above Nazan? Who has the power, can start and stop her, give her some autonomy?

Some powerful presence there must be: you'll glimpse a pair of shoes with weak flesh coaxed into them ... leaky veins piled up to finish in a leaky brain. Oh Vanity! Above the knees, the powerful are lost in clouds – their billowing clown-suits lifting with the universe's winds, their silver linings tailor-made....

'Palestine,' says Nazan. 'No – I'd not forgotten them. It's that if they stay, or if they go – not that they can, of course – it's all been tried. They don't need me, my radical cure – they need something else instead. The hand of God, perhaps, but I can't wait around for that....'

The ancestors – they suspected there was always someone higher up – angels, devils, a family dysfunctional, a mafia of affiliates, and then above them all – some thing invisible. Ineffable, says the song. Above Nazan – nothing, nothing, then the clouds, more nothing – and eventually atop it all, with compasses, some guy in exile, or long dead, or in blue jeans who shuffles to the water pot – each day the same, drink and piss; the idea that drives it all sits waving its green finger in its vase – an avocado pit that's doing well.... Pandora's root.

Irina

'Let me guide you,' says Irina. 'I'm from Nazan. She says 'We are no one, we come from nowhere ... we'll be everybody....'

'I'll show you the way, Vadim.... Relax. Our families could have made hooch together from the same still....'

'No, no,' I say, alarmed by needing guidance. 'The name's a front. My folks thought it was a protection ... might help against your guys, when they or the Americans come storming up the street. Or – whoever it may be....'

'It'll be different,' Irina says. 'It always is.'

'It's true,' I say, insisting where I know it's vain, 'Moral autonomy may seem something of a gamble. Not from the punter's side, but rather – the horse, deciding how to run, and if it wants. The state – it might have moral stature, but then there's the violence with all other states, a constant spectacle: in foggy lands, a peaty stretch of *feux follets*, of marsh gas, leprechauns, the international laws that no one knows, no one obeys .... all based on local monopolies of force, that gives each one of us the right to go to *manifs* and be clubbed....'

'Oh no!' Irina laughs. 'You start from German pundits, end with French cobbles thrown in freedom's name.... I may sound reactionary, Vadim, I speak with history's accent, that is all.'

She laughs, and hugs me. The contact's sexless, like an angel's: not friendly. Those giant wings are an obstacle ... unembraceable.

'I'll tell you all you need to know,' she says.

'Does Nazan like, love, the human kind?' I ask.

'She wants to arm it, against itself,' Irina says. 'It may involve self-sacrifice. But not hers; not right now.'

'Rather than created to frustrate her,' I say. 'We humans, we are stupid.'

'Stupider than her, that is for sure,' Irina says.

'She's lived under another star,' I say.

'Born on a harder rock than ours,' she says.

'Religion took our minds off our confusion. Science – has left us in a mess. We didn't think of how to handle things,' I say.

'Nazan starts small,' Irina says. 'Thinking she can empower....'

'Her conspiracy can rule the world,' I say. 'You're right. It's better to be with the wave than on the bottom being trawled.'

'Listen, Vadim,' says Irina. 'Once and for ever – we have a lovely friendship, but I warn you, no commonplaces when you talk with me. I've heard them all. No speeches, no regrets. No talk of love and loss – I know it all. Forget your memories of the sublime, sun on the mountains, dusk on the grass. Keep it to yourself.'

'You will pay me, Irina,' I say. 'Although the work I do is for myself, and on myself. If there's a result – it's up to someone else who's done the real hard work.'

'Yes,' she says. 'Knowing and Being – that's all the work we do. The money isn't distributed well. The more of that kind of work we do – the more we should be paid. That's what Silva did. She was paid by different opposing sources. Of course, that's very grave.'

'It's what happens to Nazan,' I say. 'She's paid by many people and what she leaves – she pays to us.

'Silva makes people disappear, she still gets paid, but not for that....'

Zelinda, lying in the flowerbed – quite unforgettable. I ought to say the episode – is 'unforgivable'.

'It's true, in a way, Vadim,' Irina says. 'In this world, you are not paid to work, you work so's to be paid. That's the nub of Marx. That's dead, of course: I merely illustrate. I study history only because it's dead. That's precisely why we militants, Vadim, spread the word, indicate the stages of a consciousness, an organisation.... If you didn't know, you shouldn't have signed up.'

'I'm aware, of course,' I say. 'Maybe it wasn't put so plain. It seemed more gradual, more tied to forms of charity, not work.... Now, it seems our work is charity....'

'It's gradual because you can't do it all at once,' Irina says. 'People do our work right, then they're paid. And in the end, *we're* there, right where we want!'

'I'm quite a pussyfoot,' I say. 'The single party.... The dictatorship ... they make me wonder ... there's the deformations that seem to come in every case, so strong, and so corrupt.... There's Nazan, inspiring – then committees, factions, public enemies, all that. Bureaucracy, then rhetoric, then jails. Dictatorship – bland, harsh, or both. The story seems eternal and a flop. Work paid, paid when there's no work. Paid to make history, or to be in it....'

'You'd better do your work, and do it right,' Irina says. 'Then it will come out as you wish. If not, then not!' She laughs.

'You want a bit of this, a bit of that,' she goes on. 'If you're not sure, and not prepared – it ends up bad. You won't get paid for work done wrong – the courthouse and the cell, the guillotine, that's what you must expect.'

'It's seldom put as well as this,' I say. 'It sounds quite stark....'

'I warned you about chattering,' she says. 'And don't do what Silva did – be paid for doing contradictory jobs. The warring sides look similar, but you have to keep them quite distinct....'

'What will happen to her?' I ask.

'Indeed!' Irina says: 'If you could answer that for anyone at all....'

'We were comrades in arms,' I say.

'Here!' Irina says. 'I'll hug you. Now we're equal, all of us. Quits. Arms all around us all! And – don't be picayune, Vadim. When the state has dropped off from history, like a dried-out boil – there'll be no single party, no dictatorship. No state. Your fear will be replaced by what you want; and what you'll get. Just do it right!'

'As a sceptic, following a perilous path – I'll end up with the contrary, negation, of a despotism?' I ask.... 'It seems a risk ... a gamble, even....'

'Anything you want or don't,' Irina says, 'is unattainable through arguing with me. I told you this; don't make me mad.... Everything you say's about you. You're a raggedy bourgeois, not a worker, not from or for the working class. I know. I've struggled to get out of it, away. I'm glad to have changed my class, my destiny, my history and future. Maybe once you knew, how everything's about class and not about the quotes. You're floating in the water because you can't stand up in it.'

'The species,' I object. 'Humanity – does not arise, although it strives.... It's flawed and limited....'

'Blame the species, then,' says Irina, turning red. 'Try being something else! A soldier-ant, a lynx.... If first you don't succeed.... Order means orders and obeying them. Lie low, if you can't accept. Otherwise – get a religion, get a revolution, get a guy who has a plan. That's salvation, Vadim, that's what Nazan offers you. Otherwise – you'll all end up in a cloud of dust!'

She laughs, and I laugh too, both unamused.

'And it could be that the mechanism works in such a way,' I say, 'that from a little brutal state, that plays the card of God, we end up with a single party, a dictatorship of no one in particular....'

'You never know,' she says. 'You live a devout, a parsimonious, life. You die; instead of heaven, down you go to hell.'

'It means you didn't do it right,' I say. 'And you haven't said what you'd prefer, Irina. What might have prejudiced it all – is your unstated moral choice. Reactionary inflections.... But then again, we're scholars, not zealots, though I guess we're in the service of Nazan....'

'It's evident,' she says.

*

'Build tall,' they said, 'and cram the buildings in. Make them a forest – solid geometry, exotic fruits – banana towers and artichokes....'

'I like these flattened towns,' Irina says. 'A single storey, and a long long single story. The wind towers, people camping on the roofs....'

'This is a risky zone,' I say. 'Elsewhere, it's sprouting still ... tall buildings ... dwarf peoples....'

'Down and up,' Irina says. 'That's simple, a perception – but it can't explain.... Not anything, except we're taller when we stand. Lichens are much much older than us – and slower too. Your friend – he looked for mystery in the horse. He had his puzzles, though he wasn't bright. Why does our horse lose, when it could win? He was intrigued – tried to make knowledge out of mystique....'

'... the horse,' I interrupt. 'He often said that's how it was for him – finding the secret.... Lichens and fungi – they were here before and now we think they'll still be here when we are not. He tried to beat the horse, fathom its mentality. The horse killed him. There's a lesson there – our inadequacy, perhaps... our wonder at things much much faster than we are, and much slower too. Legs quick, and mathematics slow. The brain, material: and hosting all that's abstract ... for us, and for the horse – memory, experience, reflection. Tracks, races, jumps. Mushrooms. Gates of perception, Irina. The death cap. On matter's map, in matter's tables, its universe – we're just a smear. A drop of blood, no more.'

'We don't have time for that,' Irina says. 'Don't meddle. Don't go down that road. Stick to the simple cycles of behaviour – humans in full fig, inaugurating, deflowering, launching Titanics, breaking the bank, dying for the king and queen....'

'My friend's search for a mystery, and its resolution....' I interrupt.

'Was naive and clumsy,' Irina says, brisk and impatient: 'And you, Vadim – see mystery in everything. In effect, in nothing. Just murk. You don't see.'

'No, Irina,' I say, 'but I have suspicions.'

We laugh, and with that we leave the mushrooms to their quiet adventures.

Nazan – where did she find Irina? Usually, there's soldiers and intelligence at her call. But Irina – is an angel. Even if you forget those giant wings, which make her walking difficult, she was fished, netted, perhaps – from some low dip in heaven. Nazan entrusted her to be my saviour. A sweet – an unforgettable thought. Another one that didn't work. But still – a treasure, a moral philosopher who doesn't push her pitch. A mercenary in the service of the good, the resolute, the burnished, heart.

I was not up to her. It bodes quite bad. I am the hero of my tale – Irina would have turned it round, and had it end conclusively. She gave me up. I settled for the grey. Greys never win – they have weak hocks, I'm told.

*

'Look!' I say. 'Piles of casings. There must be no one left.... How many bullets does it take to knock a person down...?'

'They make movies here,' she says. 'These are blanks. You can see – the cartridges are crimped.'

'Rehearsals,' I say.

'Real mercenaries,' Irina says. 'Like you and me – not metaphorically just because we're paid like everyone – but because we have the choice: we've made a choice of sides, of fight or flight, and start to penetrate the ordinariness of things....'

‘Orderliness?’ I mishear Irina, on purpose. ‘It’s so,’ I say. ‘They don’t have much here, in this village, but it’s very orderly. No exaggeration, no breaking out....’

‘It’s not a village,’ Irina says. ‘It’s a little town. There’s shops. A city has a bidonville.’

‘Mercenaries, real ones,’ Irina presses on, as we tramp up and down. ‘Take stock. They calculate reality. Engage, or a withdrawal. No rhetoric, false hopes. Our presence saves the lives of simple soldiers....’

‘We aren’t soldiers, Irina. We are observers,’ I say, alarmed.

‘That’s exactly what I mean,’ she says. ‘Remember, Vadim – we are not liked, not trusted. People want to leave, to get away. We seem to tell them “stay”.’

I’m amazed: ‘I didn’t see it that way. Nazan’s strategy called for resistance, to organise, to make a stand.’

‘Well, there you are,’ she says, ‘We two don’t agree on interpretation. It’s good we aren’t two missionaries....’

‘I thought the point was to stop the dispossession,’ I say. ‘And the refugees, but not the migrants, not at all. Migration – is the circulation of the blood.’

*

‘They know all about us,’ I say: ‘The Powers.’

‘Everything,’ she says. ‘Right now. Surveillance from on high’s the guarantee that nothing happens. They’re in the game right from the start. The eyes of God, of gods. Buying in, conspiring, countering. Paying Nazan. She knows. I know. You guess, Vadim. We’re a piece ahead of them, we’re the fox, we know a thing or two. Going to ground, doubling back. Maybe our organisation’s due to disappear, melt into something else ... be bought out, traduced.... The good guys becoming slaughterers. I spy, you spy....

'We all know everything.'

'It's not my thing,' I say. 'There's soldiers. All the states are militarised. All the powerful are enrolled. All the bosses, really super-squaddies – they parade. In uniform or casuals, elected, appointed, inherited.... Like upper servants. Dragoons, hussars, dragomen on furlough. Bulling their boots in sculleries. Screwing their batmen and batwomen in the conservatory... footmen, valets, butlers. And the lords of the manor – the frauds. Swinging their excaliburs. Charades.'

'Not so long ago,' she says, 'we superiors – might have been all on horses. To get about – coaches, even. Camels. Or in palanquins. On elephants. To carry all that armour – you'd need cart-horses.

'Then, later, when the parleying was done by servants – the chiefs still went on horseback. They weighed more, the fat-arses, but wore no armour. Smaller horses, much more elegant. Then, later still – in black, in suits, like mutes: tubercular, in hackneys, growlers.... The horse was central still. Came the durbar, then phasing out the camels, and the elephants – except to shoot the tigers from....'

'Those last big wars,' I say, 'made massacres of horses. A kind of side-show, by-blow – an unintended consequence, among the rest. What's left are museum pieces, overbred, and lacquered up. There are those that say – enough of conservation! There's so few wild things left, it's costly and contentious to maintain them, fencing off good logging space, cultivable soil ... and they've gotten aggressive too – even the former "friends of man". Not because of hunger: it's resentment. Bands of elephants, destroying everything. They don't copulate now, none of them; foxes and wolves – they're all out-bred, dropped in, ephemeral, expendable. Ignorant of nature, instinct; can't identify the awful stuff they have to eat....

'Best complete the story.... Away the big cats! Let the wild things be! Be us, and us alone!'

'If you want out,' Irina says, 'or to disappear, go underground – that's fine. We don't agree, we two. You talk to nonentities, you think it's democratic, classless, somehow it empowers. It doesn't. It's patronising, a waste of time. People don't think you're on their side – they think you're plotting. Or that you're a renegade, whose managers don't trust you.'

'Yes,' I say. 'People like us, like you – they send us round from job to job. We're in the news, then gone, gone for good. We have to write a book to be remembered.'

'Once,' she says, 'no more. You get discredited. Who cares about your memoir? You're despised, Vadim, because you can't warm blood, can't melt an icy heart. Just servile. Ill-informed. Think back – to how women are wise to you, your ingratiating sort. All those you tried to have them love you: hopeless!'

There's nothing more to say. 'I hoped to save you guys,' she says. 'But even I can't waste the time – so much, so unproductive....'

To lift her little frame, she needs huge wings and even so – I doubt the mechanics of the enterprise. Even angels have it tough – needing a tail-wind to get lift-off – when they don't have tails ... I turn my back, not to embarrass her – and when I look – she's gone.

*

I'm wrong. Wrong about everything. All those I trusted – also wrong. What comes next? A guru? Healer? Stop thinking, worrying: – cast a hook, instead, hoping the future swallows it?

When you're in an enterprise, an organisation – you've given up all outside help ... if help there ever is. Letty, Silva, now Irina – fine people, but – they're nobodies. Nazan would protect us, but she needs obedience, and if it's help you need, for her it means you've not obeyed.

Now – there's other Powers involved. We're all slaves, all of us, and we need help, and we're all spies and warriors – we don't need saving – quite the opposite.... We're in the saving business. States – just keep an eye on everything, a finger on you ... all your names.

'Nazan can't speak right now,' says Letty, when I call.

'Is it you?' I ask. There's no reply.

Silva asks – 'Where were you, Vadim? I needed you, you treated me real bad....'

'I didn't like the work you had to do,' I say. It sounds ridiculous. Zelinda – curled up like a dead whippet, underneath a flowering bush. Azalea ... good names ... only a tyro bets on names. No horse responds if you should call its name – it's you they know....

Roman

'Good to see you,' Roman says: 'I'll call the tea-boy....'

And he does.

'I didn't shout your name,' he says. 'Not wanting to advertise you.... Besides, maybe I'd get it wrong! Perhaps you wouldn't answer anyway....'

He has a crusty wart, black, on his nose end. It makes you focus. He is his wart – after a while, the rest just disappears. Is it a disguise – has he a box of them? A snaggle tooth, glass eyes: or is it an extrusion of the good, the evil? Or a device? a mike? –

transmitting, chatting to an attic in Amman? Or did it arise from some botched op? – a scorched gooseberry, juicing out from an electric poker up his arse? – fruit of a torture: him suspended on a beam by one foot, like the tarot mystic ... *l'homme suspendu,* dangling man.

'Are you watching me?' I ask.

'Professionally?' he asks: 'I'm on a holiday.'

The wrong answer.

'Most people here, from the outside, are on a business. Making or taking money. Tabulating,' I say.

'China gets everywhere first,' he says. 'I'd never stand the pace.'

I'd love to confess. Confession is a boast – to signify, stand on a scale, be weighed. Be a bad guy, or a good – not a mediocrity, an innocent. Have a significant secret.

'You're staring,' Roman says, quite neutral. 'If you hated me, were afraid – you should know I'd not attack you, not personally, not physically. I'm a no one in a no man's land.

'This is a place that's crumbling. When people know they have no power, and are precarious – others – jackals – come rushing in, not because there's strength or riches, but exactly because there's not. There is a vacuum, a territory on the slide ... suspicion, distrust and old customs, like red ants setting everyone in conflict.... Then you'll find people come from everywhere to watch, to watch each other, send reports....

'Me, I advise banks – if they should get in or out.'

'I'm one of the people here,' I say. 'I know I'm on the slide. I'm powerless, and it's good, it's sensible, it suits and fits.... I have no ambition, so I'll go down ... till I reach the firm spot.'

'You mustn't cry, my friend,' he says. 'No one should do that until it's happened. You're a delicate soul – I see that. Who's on your side?'

'Oh,' I say, alarmed, 'I have no side. I fear no man.'

'That's very hard to understand,' he says. 'Power rushes in to fill a void. Then, it flows on, till it finds another power, occupying the other shore, another territory. It hits an obstacle. Will it flood? Or be contained?'

'Maybe,' I say, cunningly. 'It's better if people stay. Don't run.'

'You'd need a backing, Vadim,' Roman says, twitching his wart. 'Supplies. A guarantee. You can't just ever do something on your own. Who's behind you, Vadim. And who's behind *them?*'

'I'm on my own, Roman,' I say, watching the twitching nose – a hedgehog's; and the sadness of creation grasps me, my head droops....

'Poor dear!' says Roman, hugging me. 'Your nerves are shot! The great design has been too much, you're overwhelmed....'

He rocks me gently, rubs my back, then – 'Maybe we should sing together. It's a healing process, makes us comrades.... We could try – something traditional we both know...'

*

> Music is a type of art, that if there is not a tinge of grief or sadness shining through, then it is not music....
>
> Valentin Silvestrov and Natalya Varenik, quoted in Peter J. Schmelz, *Sonic Overload*, OUP, 2021, p. 253, n. 162.

'What shall it be?' asks Roman. '"Rock of Ages"? Optimistic but stony. 'Lead, kindly light'? Yes, but there's light everywhere in our inhospitable and busy universe. Lead where? Kindly? Hmmm. I have my doubts. Though – it acknowledges the gloom....

'It's about wanting solidity and leadership. Do we need that, Vadim? Do we believe in that, enough to sing and say we hope?'

'I appreciate your efforts, Roman,' I say, feeling quite archaic. 'But no sex, absolutely not....' I don't evoke the wart, but there it is.... 'How about us trying "Shamsu L'asìl", "The sun at dusk"?' I ask – and indeed, it's growing dark, and cold.

'Yes,' he says. 'That fits. Perhaps too readily.'

We keen, each according to our memory, our culture, our source. His voice – it croaks.

'It can't be this,' I say. 'Some places – the *narcos* sell the forest, get themselves elected with intimidated votes, set curfews, kill opponents, kill their mates.... Where there's mines, thousands scrabble in the dirt to fill a plastic bag with shale, they fall down shafts, they're buried in the tailings ... everywhere is sold and poisoned.... It's not romance; nothing can express apocalypse, catastrophe.... Any attempt – a farce...!'

'Oh yes,' says Roman. 'This is how it is. You're in it. When these things happen, people band together – they should fight, instead they use the rhetoric ... empowerment, democracy, equality.

'Forget your sentiments, Vadim, try to accommodate to mine.... Hear me out, or you won't last; you'll run.'

'No, no,' I say. 'Let's not puff up life. That's gross. You bar your door, you're under siege.... It keeps out nothing, not the cold, the heat, the rain, the dust.... There's states, there's capital, there's industries ... just up the street....'

'And there's discos,' Roman says: 'Don't forget those. Demand! Here, there's still lots of what other people want: – even the animals .... the cubs ... the family ... cute! Rare earth for little telephones....'

'I know all that,' I say. 'But – oh misery! – if people stay where they have lived, and form militias – perhaps it attracts attack. It makes things worse....'

'People over there,' he says, and waves past oceans – 'They hope these guys stay put. They don't want migrants. On the other hand – my bosses hope they run away. It's easier to make some cash from empty space. I'm torn, you see. Maybe your bosses feel the same, Vadim....

'Better bring in an army and another state, to sort it out. The question is – which ones? Where's the best deal? Meanwhile, guys here get tired of being killed to save a hut, perhaps a goat....

'I work, I obey. I calculate, I make my judgements – the boss decides, but I've been here, I know. I've seen. The boss decides – he is a robot. He's a wired box with codes inside.

'You – you feel; you can't decide where it is you stand. You are a shade. Poor people – they'd like some resolution – you don't have the power. And so you join them in their suffering. It's you who call it suffering: that's literature. Power. That's what signifies. I have some: you, Vadim, you have none.'

'That's brilliant, Roman,' I say. 'My friend – the gambler. He had money – but no power. He guessed, he took on chance, the universe, its absurdity, its vast unnecessary expanse. He understood the root of understanding was just hazard, trial and error, opportunism – the mathematical precision of haphazardness, immense profusion; created for nothing out of nothing, streaking into nothingness. It did him no good at all, the understanding, his anxiety, ambitions. He had no handle, not on anything.'

'Well done!' says Roman. 'Too bad he's not alive so you could tell him so. But – don't stop there. If he had won, he could have changed the world, not merely understood. Perhaps you can do the next step – make something of yourself....'

'It's late,' I say, confused, dismayed.

'It always is,' he says. 'Apologies for the commonplace, but it is so.'

*

'As for the sex,' says Roman. 'The taste – it doesn't need to be acquired. Think kaki. Some people find it quite insipid – but taste is taste, it's in the fruit, spooned in. It doesn't matter whether you like it, or are used to it. It is itself. It's like good and evil: that's a fruit, it grows on trees, indifferent to you, which conclusion you may draw, or if you're somewhere in between – not good or evil. Eat – just the taste, always the same, whatever you intend. It grows on you.'

His nose....

'Growing on you must mean,' I say. 'You acquire it or you don't like it, not at all. Sex with you, Roman – a non-starter.'

'That's what philosophy insisted,' Roman insists. 'The appetite for good or bad – it grows. One or other, either, both.

'Anyway, I don't think you've been betrayed – just left by yourself to flounder where it's too deep. You don't adhere. It's good, you don't depend on anyone, but – no one cares a fig for you. You've made yourself a curiosity. You've wandered off.'

'That way,' I say, defensively. 'There's an infinity of destinations. And you, Roman – you don't propose to save anyone except yourself, your small redoubt. But you need only persons. Not a people....'

'Oh yes,' he says. 'A lover might be fun. A drinking buddy would be safer. Also fun.'

'That you can have anywhere,' I say. 'What are we doing here?'

'Here? We could take it, leave it, as it is,' he says. 'But the transformation is irreversible. The motor is inequality. Predation: the big ones versus little ones. We chase them off, we don't consume – we starve them. How? My riches, their vulnerability. And no doubt soon: – my poverty, their absence.

'You're nothing, Vadim – a project, a reform. Trees are coming, not people. No one to talk to.'

*

Nazan had said, 'You are not loyal.'

'You should be used to it, Nazan,' I said. 'It's free discussion. You change your mind, doubt, drift away. Besides, where you are liked and respected, the place you know best – that's what you most dislike, the people irritate you, you don't trust them. Then, the other side seems more attractive. Doesn't matter what it's really like. You're already there.'

*

'It's good when there's a simple choice,' I tell Roman. 'Two sides. When there's lots, you're not even asked to choose.'

'You have to make the sides,' he says. 'Then the robot decides. "Come or go, invest, or leave."'

'The people here are leaving,' I say. 'They must know more, or less, than you.'

'Nazan's coming,' Roman says. 'She must be struggling. Same old troupe. I don't think your opinion counts. She's curious about this place.'

'Every place,' I say. 'You have to be, curious about all people too, if you're not robotic. As for loyalty, Silva said, "you have to trust your judgement, not your loyalties. Loyalty is not a cause, nor an interest."'

'If you want to be effective,' Roman says. 'You have to have a faith. You have to believe – you can organise, make a plan, and that it's politically effective. Don't think you have to be a state or a messiah to bring off a coup.'

'I don't have all that time,' I say. 'Nor reading all those books ... seeking precedents will take you years.'

'And I know you, Vadim,' Roman says. 'If you have a scheme, I'll dismast you with a single puff.'

*

Nazan and Silva come. Letty has a base somewhere, anonymous. She sorts our messages. She could be anywhere at all.

'Most people left,' I say. 'The climate's poor, and gets no better. Then – there's a mine. Of course, there's taxes; soldiers – some are theirs, and others not.'

'It's vexing,' Nazan says. 'The guys who pay me – they want something clear, resolving. Some conclusions. Vadim, you're useless.... I gave you Irina, sign of the love I didn't feel – you weren't in her class.'

She rants on. Volleys of blanks. Reality resists.

'This banker guy, Roman,' I say. 'He knows how you can assess why people live on in shabby places, eat bad, survive the threats. And when they leave, he knows how to spend some cash. He knows what the chances are – to dig, to plant, to make a road, bury a pipe, to flood or drain, build a barracks or hotel....'

Roman says, 'It's true, the people here need us. If you've money or other stuff – they rob the women, and they kill the men. Then they rob the corpses. Vadim has nothing – he's a poor fish. I travel light – everybody knows. I am immune!'

'The trees here were wonderful,' Nazan says. 'I've come a distance just to see the stumps.'

'When things are difficult,' I say. 'Some people cooperate, help their mates. Others for sure will do the opposite.'

'People like me,' Silva says. 'Who're armed but have no side – we're a third force. If we wish, we are decisive.'

'Dark horses,' I say. 'Who knows what you'll do?'

'Survive,' says Silva. 'That's why the planet will depend on us. We're paid to come out of catastrophe alive, and on the winning side. We know the game – not like Roman here, whose fate ends on a robot's desk.'

'The robots don't have desks,' says Roman, quite offended. 'You open the reports, and lay them on a coffee table. Plug them in. The bosses might suggest we grow the coffee here.'

'Well, Vadim,' says Nazan. 'Your gambling friend wanted to beat the odds, do something really huge. He departed at the end of chapter one. We never know what he would do with all that tax-free cash....'

'Yes,' I say. 'It's hollow. If I wanted something big, even to fail while taking little steps ahead ... my vision would be something lasting, something that transforms.'

'I think we all have that in mind,' says Nazan, laughing. 'And of course, it's always open to anyone to do nothing, nothing whatever, just exist. Live a life, then – off! Into the mist again. Every coffin – shaped like a boat, a cruise-ship. No regrets, no unpaid bills.

'Militias or mercenaries.... Self-help or charity ... I wish I knew how it would work out. But wishing's useless, unless you hold the reins, and give the orders.'

'Wishing isn't what you mean, Nazan,' I say. 'Take Roman's counsel. He can tell you what the future is, without you troubling yourself. You won't need plan.'

'I don't ask judgements from you or anyone,' Nazan says. 'Discussion's boring, inconclusive – unless, as in my case, one of the principals has convinced a horde of people to invest. So, as regards my strategy – talk's over. Facts will judge.'

'Facts don't line up here like guardsmen,' Silva says. 'It's a jigsaw – you see the picture when you find the ultimate piece – and then you realise all has been a jigsaw, fragments making sense when all the birds have flown. You have a picture – but so what?'

'I know there's what they call "thick culture" here,' says Nazan. 'Every part of life's involved. What you say and who you meet, what you believe, what crops, what animals, what food – consume or worship.... How you react, who's friend, who's enemy.... We saw those piggy things on poles, decapitated, along the path ... that was an omen ... a tabu, a prayer?'

'Those weren't pigs,' says Silva. 'Nor peccaries.'

'Your enemies are always enemies,' says Roman. 'Attrition comes with friends, associates and neighbours. Those forever can't be trusted – the longer the relationship, the more the details rankle, the more your rage against them grows. Then – it's punishment park for all your dearest, and you are vulnerable from front and back. Your lovers turn out venomous, your parents disinherit you. Get used to life, my dears – the only episode that's guaranteed is death.'

*

I tell Silva – there's no one else I trust to tell, and I don't trust her either.

'Roman deceives,' I say. 'He's a manipulator – his reports, I'm certain, persuade the machine to make decisions that he wants. Whether the bank is in or out – it's still the force determining what will happen next ... the future. There's no plan except to give the banks the final say. After all, they'd had the first one.

'Nazan – she's naive or criminal. Maybe just criminally naive – she claims to circumvent the state by funding militias – protection rackets. People's armies. But the cash, the power, comes from the guys who are the state.'

'So, all that's true,' says Silva. 'But where am I in this?'

She serves whoever pays, and she pretends she's a decisive force. I don't say this, although she knows. She intervenes wherever there is wealth for her, and where she has some chance to save her skin.

'Well, Vadim,' Silva says, 'the people, those in need, are quicksilver. They run like ants or water – run from their surroundings and the powers.... What's your idea? Wringing your hands?

'And all your odd ideas, your compromises – believing this or that because it has no grounding and no consequence: what do they serve?'

'If I'm not attached,' I say. 'I'm still here, standing on the globe. I could call it universal, my existence, but it's inflated. Just say – I feel responsible for what I haven't done – it could be happening to me, the good, the bad ... or it's just empathy. A citizen without a state – a declaration: no one reads it or believes in it, but there it is. Universal.'

'I don't believe that,' Nazan says. 'Do we feel responsibilities, same ways, same things? Responsibility – it wobbles, melts away. I'm hungry, roast a pelican, feel bad ... but then ... you, fry monkeys every week, and like the taste. No remorse at all – where does my responsibility lead? What does it count?'

'That's easy,' Silva says. 'Enough! I have no taste for punishment, not by myself, nor anyone. You, Vadim, want confirmation you overstepped a mark you drew yourself.... That's you! Not me. I run until I drop.'

'You're idiots, you two,' says Nazan, irritably. 'I'm sure the guys here feel all kinds of things. You maybe blame the victims – probably some victims blame themselves, and others plan vendetta. It doesn't interest me, or us.'

*

'Generosity is the disposition of the dwellers in paradise....'

'Well,' Nazan says. 'There it is. There you have it. Generosity. I enable it, channel it to where it's needed. I'm not in paradise, don't believe in it.'

'Everything's complicated,' I say. 'Investment is debt, creating a dependency. Then there's who gets what....'

'Our brains weren't mean for complex stuff,' says Silva. 'Situations go back to before there was writing down. There's always been soldiers, and before that – militias, guys with spears. There was every kind of circumstance – most of the civilisations sprang from them....

'Science – there's so many of them now – we pull them out of nothing, refine them, colour them ... and yet we don't create their objects. It's all been done. Do we create them, the sciences, or are they metaphors? Can you say "we evolve ourselves"? Say "yes and no" – what do you look for then? I told you, when it comes to responsibility, it takes two ... you and who you are responsible to ... the other holds the higher card. Does that matter? What's the game?'

'My,' says Roman. 'This is heavy stuff. I thought you went for soldiering, Silva, because even if you don't win the war, you don't get hurt. And you may be decisive, but you're not a mathematician ... not everything is in your grasp.'

'It's a puzzle, certainly,' Nazan says. 'You could put it better, but unravelling it is still quite difficult.'

We look for uplift, inspiration, in each others' faces.

'You're a drag, Vadim,' Nazan says, after a pause. 'I'll call Irina. She was your outboard motor Maybe she's in reach....'

The little telephone won't work.

'I sent the car away,' Nazan says. 'Taxis don't wait in any case.... Now Letty can't come through and rescue us....'

'All our cash is in this here,' says Silva, holding up a carpet bag. 'We're not particularly secure....'

We each have a solution.

Nazan says, 'We could distribute everything, the cash, so after, we shan't be vulnerable and envied ... although it doesn't seem there's anyone to pass it to.... It's best that we don't hold the money, us standing here without a breeze to blow us into port....'

'The protocol says to bury it,' says Silva. 'We don't have a spade. And it's our asset too.... Besides, would we come back and dig it up?'

'We could walk away,' I say. 'It may be there's a truck ... even a bus ... timetables....'

'Hush!' says Roman: 'My people always come for me. Unfortunately, I don't say where I am, so they can't check up on me, see where I lodge ... expenses, all that stuff....'

It's quite convincing – no doubt he claims a sum for staying in hotels, and here, there's empty huts, for free, though they are bare.

I could have been Roman, inquiring into risk. Forming the future. It's quite my thing. But, he trumped me with the wart. To be God, you need a nose, the will do experiments, do variations.... A nose shows you are a child of God, or God.

‘I even charge the people here to touch my wart,’ he says, and starts to shed a tear and blow the nose. ‘The people here – they have a sense of where the danger is, and how to skip away ... alas, we seem transfixed....’

‘To be abandoned here,’ says Silva. ‘Without a clue.’

‘That’s so,’ says Nazan. ‘Though it’s not pertinent. My plan for charity, our discourse on the history of science and its object – those will stand, a monument for us, our reason, humanity, and our intellects. Meanwhile, yes – we’re desperate....’

*

Far away, there’s a ball of dust. ‘Horsemen!’ I shout.

‘Letty, come to help,’ says Nazan.

‘Or Irina,’ I join in. ‘Unless it’s tanks or technicals....’

It’s just dust. From the dry lake bed.

‘Lucky lake,’ says Roman, ‘to have a bed. Even if it’s dry, there’s a bed prepared and waiting....’

‘There is a scientific route,’ says Silva. ‘To deal with cash – beds too. At least – it’s mathematics. Divide the cash. Each has an equal part, and equal responsibility.... Each makes a choice – to stay or run, or dig a hole.... Stay in your own bed – be sure you have exclusive use of one.

‘We won’t ask Nazan. About the cash. She will object.’

‘No one will harm her,’ Silva says, and I remember, among the flowers, Zelinda, a crime that hovers on us all, or an accident – that passed into our memories without a lamentation, inquest, autopsy.... Responsibilities....

‘You two go on,’ I say. ‘There’s nothing here to spend the money on, no bank, no anything....’

‘The cash: it could be capital,’ Roman says. ‘As there are few of us participants. If you’re too ignorant, Vadim, give your allowance back to me, I'll make a bigger sum, and in due time, you will have more.... Sometimes, it's less, of course.'

'Suppose I'm dead,' I say. 'What then?'

'There's angels will take care of it,' says Silva, impatiently. 'I won't use violence. Nazan's silence I'll take for her consent. If she insists, I'll bleed her out – if she feels too attached to worldly things....'

We gather round the bag – Nazan's still far off, gazing at the ball of dust.

'Come on!' says Silva. 'Nazan's alone. Letty won't come – she thinks about herself too much.... Nazan has many interests to concile – in the end, self-criticism, or sharing out – it would diminish her. Let's share the loot – one of us will make it through and start a project off again ... call it her legacy....'

'Whatever you do, Silva,' I say. 'We can't get out. My solution, to leave, try somewhere else, seems the weakest one. So, we stay, and hope some people come, and we can start their world again with cash. But if we stay, of course – we're vulnerable, for sure.'

'It's Roman,' Silva says, 'who has resources he could call on – maybe, he has appointments made....'

*

Nazan calls: 'It's a revelation! The dust....'

It's gone. 'No,' says Silva, 'It was a ploy.... It made us test, display, our own philosophies. Those steeds that never pass the winning post....'

'I have the answer,' Nazan shouts. 'It's too late. It always is! It's always said: you never know the consequence of what you intend, or what you do. There's no one left, the deed is done, there's nothing still to do.

'Or else, you make your system work, and as you start distributing the wealth, you'll find you reinforce the strong. Round and round – you never catch the wheel where it is poised, the point at which it stops and waits for you to spin it on, just as you want....'

'No, no,' I shout back, across the distance. 'That's you, Nazan! You want to make a name, that's all. You live in doubt and compromise, equivocation. The cash you've gathered – we could devise a way somehow to transform, remould, the lives of all who suffer here.'

Too bad, there's only us. Too bad for me, the dust-cloud wasn't Letty, who's a second best.... Nor yet Irina – now I've forgotten why I found her quite insufferable, and how she didn't value me at all....

No one comes. Nazan stands, fixed and furious – not wanting to rejoin us, not knowing where to go.

'This money is a fortune!' I say. 'But – if divided, it serves nothing. It's a fantastic win, though it's contrived in the midst of nothing – a place of forced departure, waiting to be filled with other fugitives....'

'There's choice,' says Silva. 'Taking a vote. If Roman wants to stay, the cash will serve him well. As for me, I can pay for my promotion. Being colonel – it's what every mother wants, for son or daughter.'

'I shall be freed,' says Roman, 'to follow my vocation – philanthropy!'

Despite our plight – we laugh.

*

Three trucks come by – forests of people standing, not looking out.

'Here!' Roman shouts, throwing notes up at them. 'Take thought – there's room here if you decide to stay....'

The lorries rumble on. 'You see,' says Silva. 'Inconclusive. Nothing proved – it's quite a waste.'

'It strikes me,' Roman says, stuffing fallen money back into the bag. 'How old-fashioned all this is. Our talk of science, all that, and sex and development ... it's antique. and here we are in a true palace of antiquities.... Huts and flight! Bushmeat and executions....

'Where is the security and benevolence our ancestors foretold? The prayers! Those who stay put, at peace – can't protest. Those who're chased and hunted lose everything except their breath. And we tote remedies for what we want to change in carpet bags ... defer to desk-top robots, and talk like we were born a century ago.'

'Old-fashioned talk is unacceptable,' says Silva. 'Old-fashioned situations – they abound.'

'When we sequestered Nazan's cash,' I say. 'We took her power. Look! She wilts!'

It's true. Nazan gestures at us, silently she deflates, and squirms, hands and legs scrabble for a hold.

'Has she been hit?' Roman asks. 'A horse? Maybe it's juju, or rampaging sickness – burns your gut in minutes, untreatable and hurts like hell.'

Nazan – without her sponsors and their cash – she passes on, to somewhere we don't want to go. It helps the rest of us. A player dropping out, like musical chairs – it's a solution to a mess!

What did my gambling friend think he'd do, to spend or fossilise his fortune? No one knows – not even him. With Nazan – we think we know her plan, though all our doubts persist....

Nazan lies, eyes open, immobilised. We don't go near – maybe there's fluid loss.... She's been cut out, almost instantaneous.... What's the cause, what's to be done?

Roman's influence? the genius of the place? the sinister power of warts? It's absolutely old-fashioned, her plague, death unexplained. Where are her promises of freedom and of welfare?

The book says, one step forward, one step back....

*

'Share and share,' says Roman, 'You and I, Silva, since Vadim doesn't want to play....'

We gaze at Nazan. No power, no cash, no plot. She's at the end, bankrupted. Her last five minutes ticking out – as if the clock is speeding backwards, cancelling the pride and expectations, unspooling years with every tick and tock.

'Was it worth it? That life?' asks Roman. 'A question we ask each time. The horse – it gets you at the last. Your hands are cracked and worn with scrabbling at the walls – outside, you are convinced, there's clarity and sunshine, you've maybe made the breach at last – and then you see the dust. You never see what's in the dust. It is that horse, eyes white: lathered with its velocity, the teeth bared in extreme endeavour – it stops you, tramples you and leaves you breathless, flat....'

'Yes, yes, Roman,' says Silva: 'We all know that. But, at least the cash is left. It's up to us, it's passed to you and me....'

'In this deserted place,' I say. 'So much rhino, so much loot ... is it an advantage, that we have such a bagful, a hoard of scrip?'

*

'Lay her in a hut,' says Silva. 'That way no one can be blamed. A corpse – crawled in to die, out of the sun.'

We do just that. Nazan glares. She has no strength to spit at us. It's in her mind.

'See how the light glints on the eyeballs,' Roman says. 'It's a sign of life – not hers, alas.'

'What shall we do?' I ask.

'I'll do exactly what I want,' says Silva. 'Free will. If I'm wrong – too bad. The choice was free.'

'That's what I'll do too,' Roman says. 'If I am wrong – let someone judge. I'll listen to them, and contest if I see injustice being done to me. Or anyone at all.'

'It's far too late for religion, when it comes to choice,' I say. 'Believe or disbelieve – in what? – you cannot pick and choose. You are a this or that. Who'll tell me why I make the choice I do...?'

'That's true,' says Silva. 'It's a logical position, if indeed you choose: not like Letty, who thinks indecision is her fault.

'And – should we tell her she's to get another boss?'

'We can't,' I say. 'She cannot hear. Where does she owe obedience? The choices are all hers, but she knows nothing. She doesn't know she has a choice at all.'

'If we steal the money,' Roman says, 'we are thieves.'

'Like I said,' says Silva, 'I'd better bleed her out. You guys, I'm sure, agree. She's moribund, and we're complicit in her death, since there's no help to call, and we'd not call it anyway....'

'She is beyond our help,' I say. 'Maybe she's religious – that will change how she might see the case....'

'We should get out of here,' says Roman. 'That blood! And all our cash.... We're too exposed....'

*

We start to walk, following the route the trucks had taken. I say, 'When people need charity, it's too late. They've left, they've lost....'

'We're lost,' says Silva. 'The bag is heavy. We left – there was nothing to be left.'

'We'd nothing to say to people here,' says Roman. 'Even if there was someone.'

Irina – she always had something to say, even if there wasn't anyone to hear. Even if we could be connected up – she wouldn't know where we are ... since *we* don't know....

'She wouldn't care,' says Silva. 'I bet she didn't like the normal life; and abnormality – it breaks the chain, the bond of conversation.'

'We're lost – but can be found,' says Roman. 'The problem is – we have nothing but a bag of cash, nothing to spend it on – a liability, temptation. It's a burden. Potentially – we all have nothing except the skins we stand in. Dispossession, charity, imprisonment, and persecution – those are interludes, not subtractions or additions. In that – we're like the horse, though not so swift. We run, we laugh, we cry. Possessions are like clothes and fard. We all are Nazan, naked and dessicated in death – but just for now – we've life, and so, we're....'

'Equal?' Silva asks. 'That's like Vadim. Partially it's true, but only superficially.'

'Not being chased, I meant,' says Roman. 'Still clothed.'

And so we trudge along, forgetting, as we sweat and stagger, our complicity in murder, theft, and our betrayal of the cause. A comradeship is born.

*

'Agreements,' Silva says, 'by definition, lead to nothing, to inaction. You feel good – you're impotent. You agree to respect the Other: it's surrender. If you will accomplish anything – you must take a side distinct and independent of the rest. Allies and friends – a dream world – wake up!

'Decide for yourself!'

'I could build,' says Roman, dreamily. 'A hotel. It's a service. People move around, they meet and drink together. Hotels are benefactions. The caravanserai – how civilisations circulate....'

'I should finance the revolution....' I start.

'No!' Silva shouts. 'It must start from poverty! The Bolsheviks robbed banks – that cash, tainted the revolution from the start!

'When I've bought myself the commission, I'll finance a little army. A bodyguard: give only orders that can be carried out. That way – you always win, always survive.'

'Exactly,' Roman says. 'An Armenian like Silva knows – you're saved through arms, and not by faith. Our adventure here – it's not about the cash. It's been to reach a purpose, meaning. The future. Pushing back the spooling out of time.

'You never leave the track before the end – the last race is the clincher, win or lose....'

'Anyway,' I say. 'I'm in this with you two. I've suffered, I deserve my share. If two of us are killed, the last one standing wins the prize....'

It's hot. We must find shelter for the day, before it's *very* hot.

'Let's sing,' says Roman. 'You choose, Vadim – remember, I know only hymns....'

*

We don't hear the little truck come up behind. The guys – they could belong to many sides, or none. They could be mercenaries.

'Be tranquil,' Roman says. 'There is no dust, no horse in sight.... So far, it looks promising. We bet on each other to come through – three losers, but one of us must win....'

'We'll take the woman,' says a guy.

He and his mates look greedy, stare at her fine issue boots....

Silva has been carrying the bag. It's heavy, heavier than it ought to be only with notes. The guys start to empty it on the sand, and Silva looks undecided.... Try to run? Or join the military, these guys.... Wait to see what's weighty in the bag? Do a deal?

There must be more to it than a pass the parcel, pass the bag ... a mission, a big win...?

*

Roman and I – we slink away. These guys can't be bothered with us – and besides, we've fled, leaving a fortune, possibly, but for today, it seems our destiny is to survive.

Silva – her destiny is shaky ... bets are off.

We're not sure how it will end for her.

Soon she's out of sight.

Round Heaven, Square Earth

They paint birds – bird shapes – on the windows... pipe their cries ... This journey, this bus, is an 'as if': as if we're riding, in the open, on tireless horses ... Remember how it was, or should have been. Don't forget anything, the system says, 'Don't leave anything behind.'

Freedom – is the recognition of necessity? … the search for that recognition, how do we recognise anything? Do we enjoy it, freedom, like caviar? You need belief in the feisty couple – both freedom and necessity: – first necessity, then – when does freedom come?

No time for critics, hair-splitters, that's for sure. It's hard enough being right without defending it – then you'd ask, what it's all about, all for?

*

Rousseau – up to the guillotine, in his sky-blue coat. Carlyle said it was Robespierre – what would he know?

*

The villages full of strangers – gesticulating, shouting to each other in the street – a language not mine, but here nothing's mine anyway, no one to shout to, I don't gesticulate. I should.

*

Bus, train – you remember the unexpected revelations. The tarbrush tale … the shame: the Portuguese woman in the compartment – her husband, asleep: a greeny-brown, called 'olive', but not the fruit, not the oil. A code.

'Don't you think he's dark?' she asks me. 'Much darker than you or me.' She hopes – to make me complicit. An African, hidden in that smart suit, remembering nothing, remembering nothing of his work, his family, his language: a stranger; she must feel shame for him, the pair of him – the silent one, can't be drawn out: locked in, like a spirit in a tree. The off-white husband, who pays the shame.

*

Much easier than discovering the wheel, more productive – wheels don't build or dig – discovering slavery.

*

You don't take the bus to watch the scenery, though that is what you do. The ochre plains are painted green. My neighbor says – 'They used to paint the roses. Now it's the sand. Growing a special grass.' And indeed, he's smoking, not offering. The opium of the idle, I call pot, though now no one calls it that …

*

Better than the train – you don't need look at who's beside you, no one in front. My neighbour scowls: a tough guy. Dull and stubbly. The world seeps into his mind: this is where we are, maybe he thinks – *this is the scene, now swallow it* ... he speechifies: to no one, to the world, to his everybodies, prophesying....

'With a six-shooter against repeaters … a revolver against Winchesters in a cramped space – under the stairs – all dark, with pipes and wires, the crate of decent whisky … you get your mates to take out the guy who's loaded with shells and rifles to put them in, but he's clumsy, they're clumsy, the rifles and your guys. You keep your crew supplied, you've crates of the pistols, and in the end, they'll hit him, and your men can take some hits, there's lots of them, and ultimately, who cares, the fight is you versus the bad guys, no holds barred, except – someone must survive, it must be you, so be very very careful. But you have ammunition – don't be mean with it: even the big beasts in the box upstairs, rockets with gold and silver stars – they're there to be used in extremes, though they could bring the house down on you too. Just the sticks would be enough.

'Then it's you and the little guy – not much help expected, out in the backyard, you outgun him, but he's determined, his nerve is stronger, he doesn't have a wife and mistress, kids, a Labrador. The big guy – he fought dirty, like you; tried to stop the lines of credit: the little guy – he'll pay later, if he wins, or not at all. You keep on hitting him, but he comes on, he must wear armour, or have a pain threshold that won't kick in....

'It's decisive. If you win, as you should, you'll be top dog for ever, though you may be in a wheelchair, or if that costs too much, you'll crawl. It doesn't matter, not a bit. Who wins, they do the sums, assess the costs, say what's at stake, the values, losses, consequences for centuries over all the globe – and who else counts? Who has a better tale? So what if they have… It's flummery; too late: opinion. What matters is beating that other gang, being the only outfit in the town, being generous and mean and knocking down the competition. Losses, there are none except in books. If at the end, you stand, you've won, no one counts, and afterwards there won't be cemeteries, there'll be great plains where you can pitch a tent, take a picnic, eat jerky sandwiches. All that sand once was human bodies, your parents, lovers, you. Think, celebrate, remember – don't bother going there, it's all trash and tinsel anyway, watch the movie, they've read all the sources … actors do it better, and you see them fucking too….'

*

War and the powers – best not speak of either, use a metaphor. It's all proxy, anyway, that's the modern trick. Countries and continents – we all speak in metaphor – what we love, the tongue we use to speak with, kiss with – it's all humanized, and all that's human must be continental, you are your country, its great writers, nothing, nothing at all, except a target, like all your country and the clowns you didn't vote for and the grey junk in mines you must fight for…. Our side. You know you're on it, whatever it may be. Our species: it's you and me, and all the lines we mustn't tread on.

*

By the roadside, the signs point out a battlefield – crossed sabres, though they fought with stone axes and plutonium….

Not the great war, but a notable one, a joust, survivor forward to the next round … lots of them simultaneous, don't add together, don't generalize … Italy – battling on all sides except its own, more modest one.… Now, drifting ever further South, a pioneer in protein you don't want to eat.…

*

I say, 'Buy boots for the invasion of Russia – make the win a real winning. Finish it off – them or you, or both.…'

He says, 'We've all been told where to muster, what to pack. Spare pairs of socks.…'

I nod and smile. Playing along … outside, no fields – expanses of plasticated squares – for electricity, cucumbers? … not a soul around.

He gathers thrust: 'The last time Italians went and failed in Russia, they blamed the boots. This time – nothing at all will be to blame. Just a battle, the triumph of the wills.'

I have the window, the view: I can look out … I think, I say – 'living your life, as you can and want … does it mean denying lives to those who can't live any way at all that you would wish, that they would wish…? Do they have lives at all? Are you denying them actively – or just by living, being more powerful? If your side can win a war, those you would crush – their lives are already dwindling – fag-ends.

'Having a side, being powerful – you don't need do a thing. Just hope you're not a target. Shake the mothballs from the flags. There's people write your speeches for you, and you're loved – or not – by quantities, who you'll never know, and wouldn't like. You multiply, even when you don't go forth. Does it mean you deny … deny, by your example and your exhortations, that others can live at all? Do you see them not having what you say you value? Not having what they should aspire to but don't have and never will?'

It's serious now. He says: 'No, of course not. It's individual, life is. A spot of luck, a deeper burrow, and you're saved. It's no big deal, happens all the time. Don't fret. If others breathe but do not live – that's one thing. Not your problem, but how sad! If they're in competition with you, your lookalikes – then, you must defend yourself. But mostly – they are not. They don't imagine you. Nor you them. Your fate would not improve theirs – up or down. There's distances, and blessed ignorance.'

The passing shades of green are tiring, faded. I object, 'It's not your fate that decides. It's your power and your position, the pile of boxes you are perched on … your institutions: courtiers and arsenals. Those are decisive – if you die, it'll all have been logistics.'

My suggestion's not framed well – and if it was, what difference would it make?

Time to reward the workers? We're all poor, defeated. Mobilise everyone, everyone who's left. Russia gave up the Donbas, the Crimea – on the defensive – now's the time…? Did that happen? Decided to stop the killing, give up, retrench, accept encirclement and ridicule? Change the script. Put the workers in the army, let them eat wholesome black bread, salt fish and wash it down with home-made vodka, like your granny used to make; she called it what it is, water of life, a sea, full of fish…. You'll drown in it. Why does anybody want more territory? More people. Even your own. Relax – back to one world, conformity, stay as you will be if nothing happens. Siberia is sterile, melting, rubbing and fraying against China…. You're in a box, there is no future plan, the legacy is rubbish, knaves and traitors. Where to go? Nowhere. You're squeezed, outclassed. What's left – you're dropping down…? Try to glorify the box you're in.

Us? What's our scenario? Invade to bring true communism. Not with arms, arms can't liberate…. It's the thought that counts.

If thoughts counted.... All those peoples, languages, crammed into one immense expanse.... Then, we can go forth, make the whole world as it should be, should have been. You need stuff you can export; intricate, novel. Let everybody in, let everybody out. Forget security! No one wants you, no one knows what can be done with you.... Nothing is secure, the universe is ridiculous, a puzzle, a logical whole that makes no sense, a hole with rocks and toxic flux ... made to disappear ... forget it, no one is secure!

He says, 'You haven't understood a thing – over there, they don't live like us, don't think like us – they're robots, don't feel pain. We feel too much of it, the pain – so, everybody, toughen up! Get ready for the big one, the war, the bomb, the cancer.'

*

Once I'd make this journey looking for a job – now, I'm flitting, shrugging off my debts.... It's irreversible, and it's my turn – the last card to turn up. Rubbish. Mission not accomplished because impossible. My report – there's nothing to be donc. We've become invisible, we enlightened warriors, liberators....

Miranda organized the armies that would bring justice. Modest battalions, or a few frightened refugees. She's lost initiative. She's just the shepherd with some old shaky sheep. What next? We have no strategy, now – we've lost logistics too. This is the end. No more.

She's granite.

Something else? Not action, resistance, a camp for militants: – what, then? The press release, the squawk of indignation when the stronger side does what it wants. For me? Subversion used to be full-time – now, it's a joke. 'You rebels, you're in someone's pocket, musty, dark.'

The great quantity of jobs we wouldn't imagine doing, not for anything in any circumstance, is replaced by a mass of jobs we wouldn't dream of doing and moreover could not do. The modernity – excluding tasks involving death or slime – creates a mass of work probably greater than long ago, when we were fewer – dirtier, but less long-lived – but work is hidden in buildings, estates, ads and titles we don't even know exist.

*

'When you're not in movement, with a stranger, what are you, Sami?' I ask him, my neighbor.

'I collect insects,' he says: 'And grind them, to see what they might cure.'

'They'll survive?' I ask. 'And we'll not eat them up?'

'Think,' he says. 'The monkeys and the bears – they're full of nits – the fur, the bellies. But – there must be a plan. The Zeks, the *zecche,* the bugs, come back in their tens of thousands, unseen, unheard, underfoot and overhead. And on our feet and in our hair, and when we die….'

'Yes,' I say, 'They eat us.'

'What do you hope to do down here?' he asks. 'They've given up on growing food – it's all electricity.'

'I – we – think it is too late. The changes have been made. The bosses, proxy warriors – they've won majorities,' I say. I give him no confidences…. 'What has happened has happened in the light. The sun is hot and strong, the voices, they've never been more and never louder. Everything that happens is foretold. In general, it's irreversible, and we are all condemned, doomed. The end-game? It may make some winners comfortable, for a while.'

'All change is irreversible,' he says. 'That's philosophy. What will you do now? You're in a corner, screwed by your own analysis....'

'There's vendetta,' I say. 'There's finishing things off – symbols, designs. To find a winner – it never is too late. Besides – there's the last step at the abyss – Faust and Margarita: who goes down, who up? Heaven or hell – just a false step.... And the hero of our time – Lermontov on the precipice ... always the best advice is – shoot your opponent, don't be a gentleman....'

'Everyone has their last moment,' Sami says. 'It doesn't demonstrate a thing. Nothing at all. What you do in it – it doesn't count. The bandage for the eyes.... You could just close them, with no fuss. That last cigarette won't taste so good. And start to sing the song: they'll not have you reach the end....'

'You're mistaken, Sami,' I say. 'There's being right. That has no time. Doing what is possible – that's freedom and necessity. It must be.'

'Opportunism,' he says. 'Beginners' luck – or the last throw of the dice.'

'You asked,' I say. 'It's what I've come down to discuss.'

When they're corrupt, they can't be serious. When they're not serious – they can only be corrupt. Russia, with the Bolsheviks, could have freed a host of people ... instead, they became corrupt. The same people who ran the show from the left, slid over, did it from the right. Corrupt. A mistake somewhere in the beginning. There's only one thing you must include, when you create, lay out the earthly paradise: extinction. Your army. Created for annihilation. Force is the midwife and the executioner.

You must destroy for good, for ever. It's easy: when you break the chain, the sequence, of development, you break the ladder. Down you go. You make big snakes that eat themselves, put their long tails in their mouths and start to swallow, to digest themselves. The cycle of destruction never ends, it's mechanical. There's no alternative. Extinction means you start again, over and over, and it's always similar. And yet, the alternative would be immensely long … dinosaurs for ever. Feudalism lasting millions of years, industrial capitalism that never ends, grinds down a thousand generations. Reformism is safe and true – but you never reach the point, a goal. Revolution is swift and clean – but the sons reverse the vision of the fathers, they do exactly what they like – and they are mediocrities, slow, and greedy …. Swift to execute and jail …

I can't tell Miranda this. It doesn't make sense. Humans grew up with the dinosaurs – they can't keep to a longer path, can't make straight roads … that's what they, we, are: crafty monkeys.

Miranda protects: the camp eternal, for revolutionaries who grow old, can't run or walk. Just vulnerable. Hope they fade away, undiscovered, and uncompromised.

I leave the bus – here is Miranda. I see Sami search for his bag, stride away, not looking at us.

'It's irreversible,' Miranda says. 'What are the options? How do we conclude? Vendetta would be justified, as there's no further stage of judgement. Eye for eye, settling scores. Getting it right – finishing the French and Russian revolutions … invading Russia? Going on to China? America? Making them as we should like, as we are, as we say we are, would like to be, making them like they say they are. Making everywhere like it ought to be.'

'We could, Miranda,' I say. 'But it takes more than us two.'

'I don't know what you mean, Pascal,' she says. 'The many – always started as the few. Dealing with history, finally: me, even you. The Americans would use their bombs, but after all, they're just fragments, a people fragments of fragments. Splintered mentalities.... They've bombed everywhere, or idly dreamt of it ... planned.... They'd be hardest of all to make like they want to be. They don't think they'll ever disappear – we, everybody else – know differently. Everyone is on the slide. Whoever might survive – must be like what we hoped to be, must be like us ... like the good children we're supposed to be.... No bad guys, nevermore, ha ha!'

'What are our resources, Miranda?'I ask.

'Mojahedin, and mercenaries. We can't handle mud and snow. We could take the Southern route – Inner Asia. Our little army, unobserved, where there's less resistance, fewer people.... And on and on,' she says.

'It sounds meager, I'm afraid,' I say: hopeless, in another word. Untrue. Even with great prudence, selection, delicacy and knowledge – slink in to East Turkestan, Mongolia, then quite softly change direction ... mud and snow, lots of both.... The desolate north ... Good company, strong people, getting elderly. What am I here for? Once the plan was for a liberation, everywhere – an army of guitarists. Now – all that is sterile on your little telephone.

I say, 'The mojahedin – always too few to liberate Iran.... A necessary diversion, possibly....'

'Well,' she says. 'There it is. There we are, all of us. As the song says, people forget. Everything. Songs too.'

'When the future's been decided here, no detail can be changed,' I say. 'But then, there's all the rest ... the other continents, the sea, the mountains ... obstacles put there to thwart ... there's no maps of the future....'

'Even a losing strategy requires a plan,' she says. 'You have to believe in what you do. I'm not convinced *you* do. It's what the movies imagine you might do ... there's your belief.'

'You take greater risks in a movie,' I say. 'They have time to fill. You can try many times, and fail. In reality, the time's so short it wouldn't matter what you did.

'I ask myself – suppose we said, thinking of those huge cities, so far apart, so few of us: "End the plutocracy", and hope people, millions, would join our little band. It doesn't sound as if it's necessarily so. The risk, in a situation without a good end … is enormous and irrelevant. Incalculable. What's the interest in risk, for you and me?'

'You're here to discuss,' she says. 'Everything must change – it's just a song title. Everything *has* changed, will change. Even if there's no one like me.… I have a hope. Something will end well, although – it all will end quite soon.'

'The money?' I ask.

'Ebbs and flows,' Miranda says. 'We save, don't spend. It's dollars, naturally. Often they don't stipulate a side – the emirs, though, they want encomia.…'

'Meanwhile?' I ask.

'We farm,' she says. 'The fruits are small and hard.…'

She opens up a slender wooden house: a home, a hut, a hovel. There's buzz, activity.

'The insects – they eat anything,' she says. 'Then we slay them, by the thousands, into the pies they go, and when we die.…'

'I know, I know,' I say. 'The circle's perfect.…'

'There's circles everywhere,' she says. 'Rings round the planet, physics is full of them – even mathematics – seemed to be heading somewhere unknown to us, but now it's back, back from its trek, to ones and zeroes.…'

We laugh. I grew up here – we all aspire to be a general, modernity has found a home for us, far from the battle-lines. No sword-play now. At worst, we face the sack. Quite seldom, there might be a firing squad, but choose your side with circumspection, and there's tabu against the shedding of your blood.... At all events, the danger's from your own....

Lost loves. When you're a soldier, sex is free and clandestine. My classmates, militia-men and women – entrenched in a map of nowhere, with the contours penciled in; the ranges of artillery, radiation, the routes for refugees and penitents, the rejects and the surfeited – every taste: and none is well provided for despite the abundance of supply, and....

'Baba!' I shout. My lover from the elementary...! We hug. There's resistance – this military stuff, bullet-proofed underwear ... a turn-off for the passionate....

'We're old,' says Baba. 'No use asking where the action is. We are the rearguard now, sending out the young to be the executioners of cockroaches....'

We laugh, all three.... These are sad, bitter, days.

'You grew up in the camp,' Miranda says. 'But the highs and lows, the splendours, the disgraces – of the military life ... where are they, are they yours...?'

'It's true,' I say. 'Long ago, the whole world was at war, and organized as if it was a camp. Now – there's hot spots while we prepare for Armageddon – so, all is a camp still ... but there are tents with hoochi-koochi girls, and some with chocolate truffles free – and others where the squaddies bull their boots and dull the hi-lites on their new AKs....'

'What will you *do,* my dear?' she asks. 'Baba's a sergeant. Those are neither fish nor fowl, though they exist. But you – are nothing, nothing at all, not feather and not fin....'

'I had in mind to write the speeches, the despatches. Say if we have won or lost – and even what our aims might be. Atrocities a speciality.... The good embellished and the bad exposed,' I say.

'You might not even go....' she says.

‘It could be,’ I say. ‘That no one needs to leave their tent. It wouldn’t be a spoof, of course, but in the end – who knows? A to and fro, some insults, some sweet talk – and in the end … a satisfaction.… A dialogue, an intercourse, an interruption.… You see, Miranda – deserts have come to bore me. The mountains too, the transhumances – poor animals – bewilderment, scant food, little to wash it down … abandoned dogs, the people rushing to and fro … quite ill-adapted.…’

‘Well,’ she says, ‘it’s always so. When humans decided on the crops, erected huts, appointed bosses, priests – invented tithes, share-cropping, rack-rents and the rest – when displacement came, they couldn’t carry all the stuff they had to keep them going, so … war became endemic.’

‘The priority’s to keep the war aims vague,’ I say. ‘No threats, exterminations, no taking jobs, polluting streams. Just – an expedition. No win or lose. No barbarism.…’

‘That isn’t consonant,’ she says. ‘With what there is – depletion of resources, famines, aggressions, viruses.… Cease fire? Romantic crap! Billions must disappear. It won’t be like you say at all!’

‘Then,’ I say, not cast down. ‘An invasion under-cover. Let justice come, even as the heavens fall.…’

*

It never comes, justice. If it did, it would be painful, for us all. Invasion? The peccaries invade the monkeys’ territory, exit pursued by jaguars. Waves of migrants, armed or shoeless, bringing in power, languages, dialects, creoles and superstitions, chants and taboos and – were they peoples? Tribes, clans, settlers, wanderers, colonists – some enchanted, some bring cargo.… Where did they come from, and where are they – you can't disappear – you marry, you fuck, reproduce, leave an eyebrow or a fable for ever, it's your code.... What's it for? On the move. Somewhere to stay, to dig ... to loot, to persecute, a wooden god to shrive you for the murders and the rapes.... Where will it end, where do these people come from, layered into you, like ads, jingles – you remember the Persil ad, and underneath it – the slave labour in the factory the Nazis used to make the world so white.... Ants – the best invaders. Till they win and eat you, you can eat them – yumyum. No other food grows now except them....

*

'All these roundabouts,' says Sami. He's been listening, it seems. 'And swings. Try your strength, roll your pennies ... this is the fairground where your aim, your love, is up for trial ... try the dodgems, if they don't work, off to the ghost train.... Freedom and necessity – are written on the IDs of men of destiny. There's a special office does it: buffoons who can't tell good boots from fraud. The price you pay for freedom may be justice....

'You speak of justice as a justification for what you might choose to undertake. Desist! It's fear – fear of losing, of humiliation. Prudence. Uncertainty regarding what the consequences are, and why you start your route-march anyway.

'Those who bring justice ought to consider all the disadvantages: the disasters and the shady dealing awaiting whoever has in mind to bring a justice: a retribution, settling of scores.'

'Too bad, Sami,' I say, surprised. 'You can forget the calculation. I think we've given up invasion as a strategy for now – despite our sufferings, and those of the world that's brought to ruin....'

'Almost everything's uncertain,' Sami says. 'Starts and finishes. The only certain thing is you; that you will end. That what you hope will happen – will for certain happen just to you, as it's always been.... To no one else at all.'

'Those insects, Sami,' I ask, to change the tune....

'We'll live on those,' he says. 'Not only your meat pies – everything. We'll make them into food and clothing, energy – the lot. The horses thought they ran the world. Now – it's beasties, long-legged and not, that really will.'

'Everybody says "late capitalism",' Miranda says. 'What's to come next? If the money that we get is fruit of a corruption – the backing of all sides – why don't we make our own? Our own corruption should get us much much more, and then we'll get more people, and can think more deeply about what we want to do, and maybe do it too....'

'To be corrupt in style,' says Sami, 'you need to be a country. This "Italy", where we are's a kind of country already: it's shaky, like a memory, a dream, a ghost – people like us came here to pick tomatoes. Now, Miranda says we must turn it all around.... To protein....'

'The Mafia's here,' Miranda says. 'They're interested in our meat pies, but not in us. We are their hands, and not their brains. They're passionate for justice, but their own. We have to look outside; to be corrupted, you need big money – big plans. A scheme. Like internet: selling your privacy, your individuality....'

'Oh, faddle,' Sami says. 'Don't pretend to be a radical. Show you're open to be bought, someone will buy you.'

'I'm out of this,' I say. 'You'll suggest that we'll do anything to be corrupted. Might Russia buy us? China too? We're already in America's purse... Is this, Miranda, what late capitalism might mean?'

'You're so naïve,' Miranda says. 'We're doing something special, new. You can't use these old words to set our bounds.'

I say, 'I'm nothing in the future, not left or right. There's nothing to be, not in the future. Being alive now's like being nearly dead. All I was, was in the past. I was full of anger – that's all that's remained. The ones who were on my path, with me, obstructing me – where are they now? I don't see them. Not Sami, not Miranda. We're on unstable ground – I'm not really here, but this is it, reality. Dollars and Mafia, like it's been all my life. It's "Italy", where we ended up in hiding, because no one finds anyone here. Most places now – are Italy. Why not join the ramp? Going to rampage in Russia, then on to China, like it's always been, you must make friends with people not like you, pretend. Do your worst, make the bad better, make everything the best, and then turn off the lights. What's left will be "America".'

'We must put our hope in something that has never been, not been described, attempted, something that avoids everything past, every failure, draws nothing from them, nor from science or any data – there's a book just out in Japan, describes it perfectly,' Sami says.

I'm puzzled: 'That's a joke,' he says.

He goes on, 'You're lucky to consider yourself unlucky. You never made it to the modern world that Americans said was waiting for us all ... the Russians took a tumble for it, a Valhallah.

'And a Twilight.... It rained down tar, the deepest sins, disillusion and bad faith – into the goodness of their soul. This is the modern world, the best. A pit. We're in a blackest Africa, except we don't know how to build a hut, or a stone wall. Hold on! ... everyone is scrabbling at the slope that's nearly vertical.... But providence gave me the aisle seat on the bus, next to Pascal, the bagman, here … seller of permits to catch butterflies.… I'm the savior everyone is waiting for.…'

'I think your pitch means you can set us right,' I say. I haven't followed him.

'You can sort things out, Sami?' Miranda asks. 'Give our Iranians something – a tactical success? Pay off the mercenaries? Set us on the winning path? I'd say then – we go for it, don't you agree, Pascal?'

*

As they say, 'dead is dead', 'money is money'. We take money, more money, from whoever wants to buy. We make compromises – we abandon what would probably have failed.

There's a disadvantage. The less you do, the less you're paid. Trusted friends, they don't get paid. You must be unreliable.

*

Is it all transformed? Or just reduced. Must try harder, produce results. What might those be?

'Go and revive yourself,' Miranda says. 'Baba is waiting.…'

A touch of jealousy? We have so few possessions, the only thing we can possess is one another.…

I tell Baba, as we settle in to our familiar, distant, embrace, 'I ought to be an inspiration. Instead – I'm an internal refugee. Nothing that was can be repeated – it's a blessing, I suppose; it's all gone into memory. If you know what to press, it all comes back – in miniature and black and white.…'

Baba squeezes me, 'Nothing that was done can ever be repeated,' Baba says. 'There's nothing, no tradition, no custom, nothing that there was can be revived....' And so we pull apart, a sadness silences us both.

'When you can't go on in the old way, when the way forward is blocked – there is an answer....' I say.

'You could try revolution,' Baba says. 'Hope someone notices. There are so many, against this and that: forces without subjects....'

'Who's to do it?' I ask. 'Who are we? You and me, Miranda? Sami, who I do not know, who's taken charge, and taken cash and given it and now we're on our own?'

'All that,' says Baba, wriggling out the tent. 'Recognize necessity, and don't embroider anything. Draw no conclusions, unless you intend to end yourself.'

'High hopes,' I say. 'I came with high hopes, and now I find – the money's cut, because it's not been earned by anything; the rhetoric, some action, a general assassinated, a missile on its accidental path … all tried all gone. And everybody leaves, no one comes back.'

'Life is repetitive,' Baba shouts back. 'Sex – formulaic. The money – just paper and white metal. Stamp on the wrong face, wrong inscription – and you're screwed.... Before they left, the guys here shot off all their shells … they're old, their kids just want to farm black beetles....'

Freedom depends on the recognition … or *is* the recognition … of time, the knees that creak, the appetite that sours … losing Baba, you can't lose memories, but the memory of a loss – is loss.

'Do you miss me, Baba?' I shout.

No answer comes. It's clear – we've missed each other. End. And now? So much for fashions, sexual conventions and what isn't conventional at all. Ashes, cinders … what do they signify, except what's been burnt? That's wrong – what's burnt is gone eternally, what's new and present – is the ash.

'Miranda, we'll need a new scenario. There isn't many of us left,' I say.

'Emotions belong to the person who has them,' Miranda says. 'They shouldn't need an object. They don't transmit. Convention says – 'when there was Baba, there was love. Passion, more likely.' When that has passed – there's another emotion – not yet given its right name. If it had a name and procedures – you wouldn't feel so lost, uncertain. Sad. We're stuck to words, Pascal. When we forgot how to use them, it was a bad day.'

'… when we forgot how to invent them, so they let us see what things were for….' I say: 'Imagine – finding nameless things. A slide rule … invent what it is and what it's for….'

'Oh nonsense,' says Miranda. 'The universe is full of things like that. In fact – you'd say the universe is like a toasted marshmallow – and it makes sense. Like evolution – imagine if you had to start off designing a giraffe – much better start with something like a horse and let it stretch up to get the leaves….'

We laugh. Do we want to go further? Finding we like each other? Since there's almost no one else – intimacy? Sex or homely tales, our childhoods always at stake … maybe they're the same –

*

The danger and the promise….

'Before all that,' I say, 'we have to find a strategy for a world that spirals down. We thought things generally were for the best, and could get better. It isn't so. It all degrades, becomes more difficult, things are dis-invented. America burns up the world. You can say – cease to work, exist, be available – even if you take a horror job, you'll never save, and never earn enough so that you feel your life improve, even as your vital spark quavers and prepares....'

'Your end is not the end,' she says. 'Don't be morbid. No one will notice that you've gone, nor draw conclusions about significance and value. Think of the apples: some are eaten, some fall and rot unseen. No tear is shed in any case.'

It's true. Absolutely true. It's what they say.

She pats me on the cheek: 'Have no fear. The powers, the continents – they'll find a way of co-existing, and for sure they'll solve the difficulties they've made. They'll be giraffes. Evolution is the key....'

*

'The trouble for you, Miranda,' I say, 'is you've seen your purpose seep away: no cause and no people to be clever for.'

The appearance of things ... the taste of things, of everything – changed utterly. The look of people.... They were themselves a generation back. Now, we're on the margin: you can still be sacrificed, but the rules are changed ... a dirty game.... Those people went, and died: we are not them, will never be....

'People,' I say. 'They pull you down. They have you pity them, shift on to them what you can never do – join, enjoy, sacrifice, submit, obey, command. All that isn't you.'

'You won't be bought off, Pascal,' she says. 'I'm sure you're looking for love, at least for liking. I can give you cash....'

'Cash will do fine,' I say, and we laugh.

'Bring me more soldiers, Pascal,' Miranda says. 'I'm used to them. They don't take things seriously, they have no enemies, no rancor, and they manage fear, their fear. It protects them – you put it in your pack and when there's danger, you're afraid, you run. It's service issue, you have to have it, packed away, in working order. It's useful, fear....'

'Essential, I should say,' I say.

'The snow here, that's all that makes me anxious,' she says. 'The winters are short but very sharp.'

'Most people try to act like soldiers now,' I say. 'Some talk warlike, as if it's coming, but there's war everywhere, all the time. It makes no difference to anything, talking tough.'

'These are ancient qualities,' she says. 'The lords were brought up to them, the counselors – the duelling in the atrium – the warrior monks, the princelings. Civilisations where no blood was shed – all the heirs were wrapped in carpets, trampled to death. How do you drill for that?

'They saw it all as battles. It was dull. It happened when the harvest finished, every year, manoeuvres, billeting, rapes and thefts. That's why they invented the machines – robots for training, for making cannons; keeping people occupied. For marching.'

'I'd like to create something magnificent,' I say. 'But even victory's a disappointment – the money spent, hospitals overrun, and all the rest. There's a parade, and that is it. The boyars in committee – they talk big, but they weren't there or anywhere. And everything is smashed.'

'I could be a warrior,' she says. 'Take ship for vengeance. First, be a soldier. Then – try making love. Start a new species – I, with two eyes, timid, steering through the rocks; and the crew with that awful disease – left with one eye....'

'One eye between them all,' I say. 'One person could invade. More would mess it up. Swim lake Baikal, catch fish and salt them ... a paradox, that. Fish should be salt already, but the lake's salt-free, that's why it can happen so....'

'It's not at all like that,' she says. 'They lower lamps on ropes – the fish swim up, they think it is the sun – the pressure lessens, up they come, and they – explode! It's quite unique. They built a railway round the lake, just to watch....'

'Is that why there's nothing left at all, in the sea of Aral?' I ask, joking. 'All fished up?'

'Just think,' she says, 'moving millions – from Stalingrad to Berlin, decisive shift – and now you want me to spend years, just making love and raking sand!'

'At least you see how complex it all is,' I say. 'Even as it comes to an end, a halt at least. Does it freeze, or does it disappear? "Making love...." – like making pots, the potter's wheel. Not love at all – just reproductions. The sea makes waves: succession permanent.

'Sex – I make you – do you make me? What do you make of me, make me do?'

'Exactly,' says Miranda. 'We have no desires. Did we have them, or were they holes in the landscape? They are no more, not had, not missed. Desires were our gods. We don't believe in them, the gods, because we never got to them. They help us in the battle, so we thought – but then, all over, finished, we were back at sea, seeking someone who would satisfy desire....'

'Who would *embody* desire, Miranda. Witches with snouts – there was no limit, your seat was free, but in the end ... you had to row, or finish in the drink,' I say.

'In the end,' she says, 'we were right, not wanting to leave home and go there anyway, all that blood, the gods, the heroes – the party – all the members, dull, extravagant, everyone, all cut down.... Troy promised, but an illusion. How tiring! At last, a king-size bed, and off we go, the land of Nod, the sandman cometh and drifts over us....'

'I may as well do the invasion on my own,' I say. 'If it doesn't work, I can deny it all.'

*

'They say time is the cruelest. Ageing,' Miranda says. 'Yet time is always having new ideas, always rejuvenated. Without time, there would be nothing new....'

'"It's true," I say. 'But poor Baba! A wreck. Like the giant who wanted to eat everything, and went to the Himalayas, and, like us, gave up....'

'Well,' she says, 'what do you suppose I'd look like? Say there was the old me, young again – and the new me, but old?

'Me, the adjutant of a camp of guerrillas. Invisible – my void, my hope. Well turned-out. My mountains? All scoffed, swilled down.... How many massacres have I avenged!'

'I've no idea,' I say. 'I'm just a publicist. I travel round, promoting you, to stop you being discovered. This country is full of settlements of slaves and warriors – all hidden, all maybe useful for if the broken time-piece strikes.... I know you're on the winning side, the good. It's to be expected you will suffer setbacks. I got you more arms, up-to-date – it's natural, that people get older, incontinent, they lose their direction, waver on their legs, exhaust their arms ... are toppled over by a single shot.... They forget, repeat themselves, try to concentrate, but you'll find, it's going back to their beginnings – a sign of dementia.... That's an obligation. The guns are on automatic now – it's remembering to plant the seeds, you should get a notebook, write the word THINK! And that should be enough....'

'Look at me,' she says. 'I'm all I was when I was young, but now I'm old as well. Two for no price – I'm the one you'll get for free. Your problem is – I don't much fancy you. You're not the problem, nor a solution to anything, that I can see. You don't stand for settling scores, nor yet for continuity … you just stand there, unarmed, unloved. No fucking use to anything.'

'It's never been my job,' I say. 'I'm there to know it all and try not to have them find out who you are. Besides, you're no longer what you are. They've gone, you've gone. Farewell to arms and legs and intellect. Now you want me to find another bunch, another army. It's late. I found you lots. Where are they all?

'I told you, it's time I set off on my own.'

'Before anyone sets off,' she says. 'We must get things straight. We won't go to America – there is the sea, and they are organized to kill us all. Now, Pascal: freedom. The goal. Be clear. Is it rules, or against them, or just opportunist – keep some, break some? That could be the essence.… Then – necessity: what we have to do, what is advantageous to do, or what the past makes us, in the present, do?'

'Well put,' I say. 'And even if you make conclusions from all that – what are you trying to achieve? Freedom? Or quite something else, something we can all enjoy. Free education? That's not freedom, evidently. Most education is about rules you must obey. Mine was about dance and movies, graffiti – not freedom, not at all, but fixed on evading rules as far as possible, and often into jail and bankruptcy, muscle strain and linament. Humiliation, Miranda. Ridicule. I'd been convinced it's freedom. I am still looking – but it's not what you'd seek if there was otherwise.…'

'Let's try this,' Miranda says. 'Invade everywhere, one by one the places, by both of us, since we've no resource, no reserve. Like a virus – kill or cure.'

'And where's the cure?' I ask. 'They won't know they've been invaded anyway.…'

'*We*'ll know,' she says. 'And things will change. No one knows why one thing changes everything, and others – end in silence, or in the folder "no one knows".'

'Invasion could become quite fashionable,' I say. 'Like giving bio-samples, then regretting it. All is exposed – and then?… We could start a movement – invasions on a massive scale, by individuals – no longer tourists on a bus, but you and I. They say a drone is a computer than will drop a bomb on you. We're not a bomb, we're better, we can be used for lots of things, we don't explode, we go on and on, we don't take orders, but we can, we can! And no one will ever know what orders we'll obey and what we won't.'

'Now,' Miranda says. 'We have our plan. You thought because the warriors had gone or died, forgot their skills … rheumatic shoulders and arthritic hips – our mission had expired. It isn't so; that's clear. Let's sort through these old documents….'

She brings out a bundle – passports of the dead, visas, deportation orders from everywhere, museum passes, tickets to a coronation or a funeral.

'Take some of these,' she says. 'You'll be on lists, and some are forged, on some you look like ghosts. Be careful how you use them, where, how often – you see, Pascal, you thought not having documents had made you vulnerable. Now you see – too many mean you need to know the world minutely – where you can enter, where they will have you disappear; where you can't admit to having lived….'

'Invasion means you can rampage in and kill and torture who you want,' I say. 'And change a government, like a democracy or a revolution is supposed to do. It all sounds trivial. Yes, when we look back, invasions also, mainly, mean amalgamations, changing cultures, shifting from empire to asceticism, religious bigotry to syncretism, writing left to right to right to left … counting in twelves, then to tens or fives….'

'It's a puzzle fit for monkeys,' she says, entranced. 'Planting peas in rows, carrots in clumps, a national sport of climbing trees or digging holes – all can be upturned, inverted – all that made you citizen and normal – changed. Changed totally. Custom, tradition, normal and normative – erased, replaced. Your intimacies, your superficialities – changed not by haphazard, by pen-friends, by messages and games – but by people, determined, trained, walking among you – not spies or kidnappers, but Pascals, Mirandas … you and I.'

'What you say is true,' I say. 'Enormous. But shapeless and inconclusive too. It happens all the time, and yet, the more it happens, the more people prepare for war, destruction, to stop it happening at all! To stop it happening by foreign states, the state you live in, and yet … it happens…. And yes, wars happen too, all the time….'

'Even as everything changes,' says Miranda. 'People convince themselves it's all about the warriors, artillery: digging latrines and singing round camp-fires….'

'We're going to invade, Miranda, 'I say. 'Everywhere we can. We can't be superficial. We must decide what's special about our invasion, what we leave, what we transform. What we bring back and what we tell. The absolute, the Marco Polo gig….'

'It's a special adventure,' says Miranda. 'A first, a one-off. We'll walk, appraise their monuments, eat their borshch, their noodles and dumplings, and whatever anybody eats elsewhere. America – dry fatty stuff?

'A flaming vindaloo, perhaps … nasi goreng … pet their cats, talk to them: the sort of invasion that happens anyway, but without the napalm, the Agent Orange, and the graves….

'We'll profit from their humanity, if they let us peep inside. That's all....'

*

'You can't do that,' says Sami. 'There are contracts, there are debts.'

'We can't pay,' I say. 'Having no cash. So, no soldiers either. We might receive it, but not pay it back. Besides – no one of us would ask for cash ... if we did, it was without hopes of profiting or owing....'

'Oh yes,' he says. 'Someone asked. *I* did.'

'You shouldn't have,' Miranda says.

'You wanted cash, like everybody does. Now, your invasions,' Sami carries on, shrugging Miranda's hypocrisy to one side, 'Stupid as they sound – where do they fit in? Is it to tart up your biographies, when everything has failed?'

'I see this as a freedom,' she says. 'Us; spreading ourselves, thin as a skin, with no hostility. They, listening; with no defensive stance. It's a necessary gesture – there's necessity to exist, to change, and be transformed in turn. That is invasion, Sami – over and above what can be written down, contracted.... Invasion. Time, change. Resist time and change; you change, you age, Time comes. And passes, but – all is changed....'

'You must honour our word, Miranda,' he says. 'Not run away.'

'It's a farewell, invading,' she says. 'Whether you leave, or settle in. It's not like starting up a fashion. Where you came from – unrecognizable!'

*

Two guys from the beetle-houses escape, come and give Miranda, me too – a kicking. It breaks you, your mind, your faith, your hopeful disbelief; some parts are not replaceable – the offal for the cats, liver, kidneys … your lights.

They're well-set types: young, agile. Well fed on beetles black and green. They make an error – finished with us, they run across the road, get stopped, and beaten bad – much worse than us. Security pounds them, like they do for slaves or convicts.

I'd like to apologise to them, but it would be mad. Not welcomed, either. If there is fault, it lies with Miranda and myself – and Sami, who'll have tipped them off and set them up. Set us up as well.

Now, I see where necessity lies. Soft shoes … boots would have killed us. Necessity means 'submit' to what there is, but you must recognize that tough guys don't get issued boots. Do not kill – that might mean trouble! It's all necessity, for other people; but it covers you, does you good without intending it.

*

'We can be whole and pure, useful and lawful too,' I say. 'If we accept that Sami is a spy of sorts, an entrepreneur, and if he has his way, we could end up as farmers of the crawlies.'

Or else we run, and think of other things to do when we've escaped.

And that we do.

'We trusted Sami,' Miranda says. 'How can we judge him now?'

'For sure, we had offended him,' I say. 'But he knew us. We were true to ourselves, our situation. True, we let him down, his judgement, his commitments. And what he did was inexcusable....'

'People are like that. Think of Trotsky in the Blue House,' she says. 'Defended – but by inattention.... He could be exasperating....'

'That's not how it looked,' I say. 'Maybe they were tired of all the infiltrations – they were used to board games, not killers....'

'The secretaries were his bodyguards,' she says. 'They dropped their guard, then there was just the body. But after all, he was spent.... Spain, the war, that was the end....'

'In Sami's case – it was a treachery, a plot. Forget Trotsky. Sami bargained for two desperate guys to beat us up, exchanging for their freedom, which they didn't grasp,' I say.... 'They didn't know how to reach out for it, and were left with us two beaten, then it was their turn. No one with anything to show. Sami – some empty vengeance. Defeat all round, unnecessary – defeat was here already. Sami was scum – he plotted a punishment irrelevant, which could have left him with a murder rap....'

'On commission,' says Miranda. 'He'd get off. Grass on your mates, and have the killers eliminated. On and on, leaving injustice ... spreading like rat poison on your shoes....'

'It's an English movie,' I say. 'A Hitchcock, interpreted in France. Grand Guignol. Madness and violence in confined circumstances. French people have the guillotine as last resort. The English prefer treachery.'

'You brought Sami here, gave him your trust, our information,' she says.

'No,' I say. 'He was on the bus, he knew everything. He wanted to tie you in – the money, the powers. Americans. That's who he represented – maybe he misunderstood "invasion"....'

'Of course he did,' she says. 'Invasion in my sense is pacific, it follows circumstance, it's not a campaign, a military thing that needs finance.... It isn't bland, though. Not tourism. We bear a message in our gaze, spread it, take everything in. No one – no autocrat, no general, no oligarch – can do more than that. We've no resources – but, you'll find – resources slide away. Pouf! All you ever have, when you invade, are eyes and feet and brain. That's all we have. We don't loot. Sami must understand....'

'It's not at all where he stands, what he wants,' I say. 'It happens like that, like you say – like pool balls, we're all round but with different values, different colours, same destinations, same disappointments. Often in balk. Some are Buddha, some are Genghiz. Some are us two. It's not so hard to understand.'

'My family's still in China,' Miranda says. 'Fujian.'

'I've always thought,' I say. 'The Han. They are my people, like my people were, only livelier, except they've probably changed as well, like my people changed.'

'I didn't know how sentimental you can be,' Miranda says. 'I wanted to try new things. It's very hard – you end up in someone else's campaign, it isn't new at all, it's just what everybody's doing, and those that aren't don't care, or look down on you.'

'That doesn't sound so terrible,' I say. 'There's worse. I got reported, put on a list. That's why we never get to leave, and people desert us. Desert me.'

'We're leaving, Pascal,' she says, determined. 'And those lists are longer than the world has lived. Anyone with spirit is on more than one.'

'Rites of passage, Miranda,' I say. 'Where you're supposed to be going – who knows?'

*

Yaroslavl', Chelyabinsk, and beautiful Sakhalin

It's a long trek, but we make it, us two. Hundreds of cities, towns, hamlets, settlements – perhaps thousands. Quite exhausting, the human condition – everywhere we live in packs, in herds, and yet the isolation … the silence around us; no one says 'you're not right, you're sick, your mental state is compromised…' until you flip or die, and your family puts you in the Isolator.… You're loved and cherished, then you're not, and down and down you go.… People disappear – the Vjatich, the Krivich, in Russia before the Mongols, but not Russians – or else 'true Russians', who have disappeared. Make the choice. They disappear – but they are there, for always, like the Kushans, Huns, the Sakas. Present but disappeared. Countries and continents – changing shape, sinking, rising in flames and buried under ice. We invade – no one feels a thing, just like they don't feel the future or the past – it's in the head, like dreams and fancies, and all the others, educated as Russians or Americans, but not.

'The good times,' Miranda says, 'where they make a fuss of you, take the jars off the shelf, wondering what's in them – pickled … often the people are pickled too.' We laugh.

'Sakhalin was spectacular,' I say. 'I hope no one but us discovers it.'

'Of course,' she says. 'You never discover anything but yourself. That's trivial, and so – a sortie like we did is what you do. A walk, a stroll. Trivial but devastating. Route-marching on the map, the atlas. That way you find the world is small and round – maybe you knew it all already. China will be like that too, I'm sure. I've seen it all, like Marco Polo did … the kingdom of women – should be Queendom, surely. You take the bus. Too bad they had a monarchy – you imagine people being free, but, you get it wrong.'

'You've seen your part of it,' I say. 'Living and moving round. I'm sorry your family let you fall to pieces....'

'Oh,' she says, 'pieces is all right – it's when the whole lot tumbles. I was boss here, cruel and demanding too, till you and Sami came. I ran the show – better all the time, until it was a monologue. Now – invasions. Another time, we'll see Baikal....'

*

Lanzhou, Linqing, Linyi
Baltimore, Billings, Bakersfield

Miranda wrote them all on a white blackboard – then we invaded, came home. The names were still there – so were the cities. We didn't loot, or deface monuments, knock anybody down – indeed, we didn't profit from all this. Did the inhabitants? Hard to say – it always is, and usually it's left to history, historians unborn, unknown, to make assessments. There are tens of largish countries left we didn't invade, and no one else would think of doing it with military force, although there's motives for doing it to most of them, one way or another, with our side or someone else's....

'We don't believe in peace at any price, nor war, nor do we need believe in anything at all,' Miranda says. 'Invasion's not like that. You do it. Then you see. Or, if you don't see, history will judge. What we did was right – a surface barely scratched, and all the places starting with other letters left alone for now, although invasion will strike them as well, and everywhere will take the lesson – for there's no defence; and if it isn't us, it will be someone else.'

*

'You stole Baba,' I say. 'I look back, and there's my red anger.'

'It wasn't sex,' Miranda says. 'It was to make you both more productive. Stop thinking about yourselves, think about me, think about world revolution – or at least, stirring the pot.'

'Those weapons won't end it all at once,' I say. 'The rich will disappear quite quick, then it's the rest will grind away and suffer. You see, the weaker, the male – has to start it off. Those bombs are a temptation – to see how far you can resist – if they work and what they'll do. The comic books have shown the ruins, but that is fiction, unbelievable. 'How would it be if?… Suppose…. Suppose we bomb everywhere, the world. We're doomed so's all the rest. How frightened can people get, what will they do – scuttle? Where to?'

'The weaker – they've a staircase to go down, steps after steps, some you could use to climb up, get some respite, a better view…. The loser has to tell the whole story, end the parade, shoot the horses, overturn the coach – end the species, its charade, its rules, its laws and all the players – clowns on stilts….

'You start the epic with a trial, a sighting shot, and on it goes – your city pancaked, then it's theirs goes down … the rivers, the villages, over and over, it's all a ploy, a play – a band of jackdaws swoops to take their queen, and then it's yours that's beaked, and all the while the soldiers drop, are bulldozed into pits, and then it's you and grannie too – who comforts who, and who believes there is a point where someone's interested to see the chapter end? How we loved the inequality, where some could sing and ride on swans, and screw their fellows and invoke the destiny designed by God or gods or by the markets where you sat for days and tried to sell your dross…. Death's welcome when there's nothing left to do, and someone tries to kill you so there is more room for grazing and for growing weeds….'

'We're curious,' she says. 'Keeping those missiles in the sheds until it's birthday time and out they come and trundle down the street – it's just too much. Fireworks. The names – niggle at you. Golden Rain, Roman Candles – Jupiter and Big God. Send off a few, and see if the bang is big, or even bigger than they say.'

'Cities with a million – how many? Guess – five hundred. One a week,' I say. 'They'll titillate. Death and the pictures, the laments, distress. They'll do it slow. Ten years, and then the rest, and all that's been hidden – just to blow up, all of it, the dull stuff, the innocence – things that stick nowhere, to no surface, nothing to do but run their course. Destroy a city – nothing. Gone utterly. As if it's unfindable, because it's changed its name. Cities in the sand. Five hundred epitaphs – a prize for the best slogan, song, or metaphor. An epic? A chapter to go, in your "Time regained" – enough you put some sticky paper on the windows, euthanise the dog – you'll live to finish "Looking for time", and start "The Human Age…." Die after decades in harness, not for you the dog's end, off the cliff, into the tip. Upright in your chair, a poke of pot-noodles ready for when the muse logs off…. Natural causes. What else?'

'Nothing to fear, just fear everything, as we've always done,' she says. 'Everything there was that could find refuge, we saw it through: the scissions, the renegades, anti-imperials, anti-fascists, anti- and anti-post-colonials, anti-authoritarians, Leninists, Maoists – every variant that could be invented.'

'And if it wasn't invented?' I ask. 'You, me – we had no say in anything.

'We wanted to change things – now, the world's protesting that it's all too late. Do we belong here, hosting a million to demonstrate for food and water? It isn't us. We're finished, Miranda. Politics has changed, we haven't.'

'Assassins,' Miranda says. 'That's what Sami has in mind for us. Another hit squad … our role.…'

'There's no room in that field,' I say, appalled.

'I know how to get the hash,' she says. 'It seems you must be quite spaced out, if you're in that line.'

'Oh,' I say. 'I'm sure they didn't use. They traded, probably. They had this fortress – impregnable, they say, but they never are. If they smoked – it was to go deeper in. Religious. Gates of perception, that kind of thing. Deeper into somewhere, something.'

'The people who came here, Pascal,' she says. 'To train, to hide, to plot and plan. They were delightful, but not pacifists. Resistance, armed struggle.… You knew, and everybody knew.'

'And it was good and just,' I say. 'But now?'

'We must decide,' she says. 'Next. But quick.'

'You were so welcoming, Miranda, so convinced,' I say. 'Of everything and its opposite.'

'I was consistent,' she says, huffily. 'Persecution, bullying, fighters for freedom – yours, mine, their own. I was a hub.'

'Leave or die,' I say. 'There's been few people here for many years. It was over when you started – religion and fascists. Not your thing. There was the old guard, if you trusted them. They would come, but generations had already passed – millions might appreciate you, but few did.'

'So be it,' says Miranda. 'Make your analysis. Everybody does, the grind goes on.'

*

'Elephants,' I say. 'I know the rats will all survive – if not them, then rats identical. But elephants – they seem so distant from our frivolity, our need to mate progressively, to argue and find fault.

'The trek. That is their life – their delicacy, resignation – determination. Everything we have evolved out of ourselves….'

'Do I spot a tear, Pascal?' she asks. 'I thought only elephants were tearful – the small world they live in, everything in it stamped into memory – we make ours big and bigger so we don't need to mourn, to miss, to like excessively….

'We need a bell to tell us when our friend is dead – I don't think elephants would need one….'

'There will be someone doing what you did,' I say. 'Somewhere else. All I supported and was discreet about … what everybody knew… And now – no one feels safe … no one has secured their integrity….'

'Are you with me, Pascal?' she asks. 'Wherever I am, wherever else we go together, are you for me, on my side? That is love, you know.'

'Is it?' I ask, overwhelmed. 'It's much further up the scale than I can reach….'

I've been committed – devoted, even. I – we – had passion for Baba, but Baba aged, became an other.

'They say,' she says. 'That in the end there's only love. All our effort, efforts from all sides – the cheats, the lies, the snipers and the torturers – and is it all for love? To end in it, nothing more? They blast the mountain ranges and what emerges? Love: the rat! And is this all, love? The rodent?

'Vietnam, Algeria – it fired me up although I wasn't born, but it was news. The news, always repeating, our side is winning – except we were the enemy! We were the underground, resisters who could not speak, invisible. A plot without a point, without a character until – there was another lot, another provenance, and more and more, people, my kind – escaping, running, staggering, and nothing I could do except find them a refuge while they wondered where they'd go, who'd take them in and if they would go home, ever, ever, "roses, roses" and live out in some desert space a history they hadn't made: tales, stories, and the victories, processions, ceremonies replete with lies and puffing, till they're settled in the chair and pushed out in the sun before the hut to simmer and to die.... I am nothing to them, and I loved them....'

'Love?' I ask. 'It's desperation. The last breath. Things are tough. There's more and more spies – whenever you write a note, you don't know who gets to read it. More important – is the cash....'

Sami has access to cash. Love, they say, requires no reciprocation, no reward. Money: given selflessly, can't be stopped – not refundable: just like love. Makes you do silly things.

'At times,' Miranda says, 'I realize I've nothing. I've fought my battles, but that's it – they weren't for loot or glory. They weren't even battles, and there was no outcome ... not one I wanted. Doing right – that must count for someone.

'Sometimes, I think you don't like me, not at all, despite our very long association....'

'That could be so,' I say. 'You're oppressive, demanding, obsessive. What you want cannot be attained, because it's full of contradictions. You don't see them. You must settle for disappointment, or prepare a change of side. People, your people, must take power – you'd like them somehow to give it up, or use it as it never is ... and if they did, they'd have to start again. Justice is hard and cruel, freedom is narrow and besieged. Power is malign, vindictive. Love is....'

'Something we all know,' she says, 'and talk about. Cash. What's left, that you can spend. Love. Remembered, contradictory, indecipherable and incommunicable. Emotions are not beyond discussion and understanding – it's that we drift and spiral like feathers from a vulture's wing.'

We leave it there.

*

'Is there an erotic charge,' Miranda asks. 'In bombing those big cities? Erotic cannibalism: – one of my warriors left a video – it was meticulous, but not exactly clear what was the point of view.'

'It's not the way to go, Miranda,' I say. 'Desire of the Other – do you think you eliminate the Otherness by consuming it – if you could consume a concept, a *Begriff*? Or do you make it part of yourself? If money is shit, to spend, you could say too that all you eat is shit, the process. Money – was your food, and now.... It means Eros is your desire to consume, eliminate. The feast, the potlach, is the place where generosity, excess, creates occasions for loyalty, securing the dependences – a contempt for the inferior.... Evacuation.'

'I think you're moving to an answer "yes",' she says. 'Destruction and desire, how can they be separated? It's occupation and invasion, just as we did, the whole world – was our oyster.... And did it shriek as you gulped it down, Pascal?'

'A little learning, Miranda,' I say. 'An excess of theorizing on your part....'

I'm embarrassed by the swarming bees I've released.... Maybe it's so – eating together, eating each other, an intimacy ... and then – elimination. The other side, the secret pact we make with ourselves, to join the other, but still be separate. A fiction. The brotherhood that's murderous love ... the treacherous arrow – Baldur comes to mind ... 'the family that eats together, prays together' the Sunday roast, the wine, the flesh.... The ritual where you eat your enemy, who becomes a part of you....

'Baldur – more beautiful than a thousand suns,' Miranda says. 'Killed by disorder, his destruction leads to a new race of gods....'

'We can't go there,' I say. 'Humans are simple artifacts – flexible, like a screwdriver that can put out eyes or force a lock. We think because we're fluid, multivalent, that we're sophisticates. We live in metaphors and parables. We adapt to almost everything, and so we think we're lords of circumstance – it isn't so. We have no meaning. We're not for anything. We're ragged monkeys scouting for road-kill … bush-meat, *carogna*.... Some bands are well-equipped, inventive – they kill with great success, and film themselves, they moon and chatter. Just monkeys: what can you expect?'

'Exactly so,' Miranda says. 'My giving refuge to the persecuted was obviously ridiculous. I should have served them up on palm leaves to their comrades, and the manure would make a garden wonderful … a paradise … good and evil on the branch … talking reptiles versed in ethics....'

'We ought to leave,' I say. 'The atmosphere is heavy here. The deaths of all those beetles and the long-legs – there is a reek of blood, of wriggly agonies....'

'Remember,' Miranda says, ignoring me, as I try to evade the unresolved, the weighty anti-climax. '"Why do we desire the good?" That was a question with an answer set out like in geometry, with triangles. But the good – does not desire us. It is always we who desire – we both desired Baba, Baba was indifferent. It's us – love: our love of beauty, titillation, acclaim. Desire – of good or bad. That's desire. Desire is what you feel – there's no boxes in the grass, one labelled good, the other bad. If you desire a box, you go for it. If not, then not. Or pick indifferent – or the bigger one.... It's the surprise, the desire, the appeasement, not the label.... You desire the box! If you don't desire the good, but practice it? And what if you desire the bad, and it's reciprocated. Tequila's desired, and it is good, next day it's bad, and yet it isn't there, it's only always you, your head, but try again … and so, and so …'

'It's easier, Miranda,' I say, exasperated. 'If you use different words. That's what philosophy concluded, and what concluded all philosophy. Desires are subjective, there's no objects, only states…. You gave refuge to those guys because you disliked persecution, for yourself, and out of empathy, dislike of pain because you understood exactly what and why it was … you had a view of humans that preferred each one to have a personal field to cultivate … with a minimum of pain, avoidable … a guarantee of space without incursions or controls….'

'Less necessity,' she says, seeming to agree. 'Or different sorts of it.'

'And that you thought was "good",' I say, hoping to conclude.

'Listen, Pascal,' she says, fired up. 'Women. They should not get guns. If you can stop them – do! No guns, no lead pipes, no cleansers – even no matches and no lighter fuel.'

'They don't come here,' I say. 'Those women. You'd welcome them, I'm sure. This place – it has a military mien, of long ago….'

*

Desire. The Greeks, the Indians – they knew desire was enough to destroy their world or make it into shapes defying the hypotenuse. Fertility? No, just intercourse, not novelty, just variation, a prime of seven figures … possibly…. Spend your life looking for the highest prime, the unsuspected novelty....

Inventing the zero – signifying nothing, yet permitting everything advanced – the length of worlds and universes, the symbol of desire forever unappeased and inexplicable, indivisible. Miranda and I sleep side by side, like Etruscans in the tomb, on palliasses in the wooden hut.... I remember those ancient buildings in Bukhara, of stone and brick so carefully rendered as to resemble wood – the wood the earlier buildings were built from. Two steps forward, three steps back....

Leave nothing behind, remember everything, remembering the beginning and you'll recognize the end.

A hut like you could buy from catalogues. Creosote, always a retsina smell. And wondering – if it is all desire, some good, some bad, but always desire – wondering if Miranda has in mind to eat me in the dream, if I could sleep, and wake up covered in the blood of what? – a succubus, Miranda – or myself, devoured, transformed ... and Baba standing somewhere 'on guard', as if the persons to be guarded weren't us three....

'I slept bad, Miranda,' I say. 'Thinking of the cops. Intelligence.'

'Oh,' she says, 'they know everything. The people here were refugees, had a document, with asylum. Not wanted. Offensive. Best have them settle. The cops can trade them, betray them, expel them, extradite them, send them for trial, have them assassinated, or use them for themselves. You could say I was complicit, in a way. "I know you know I know" – except that you can't admit. Not anything – even "mum" is not the word!

'Now we've invaded everywhere – they might leave me be. I'm a known quantity. I don't take cash. You, Pascal – you're grey. You have a reason for doing everything, and its opposite. You're an opportunist. I prefer Sami – you know where he stands, and he could change, change utterly. You can't.'

There are no objects of desire: there's just desire.

She takes Sami's money, that's for sure. With Sami – you're nowhere near a true opponent – he's just a tempter, a siren. We're used to ending on the rocks. What has she to give him?

Lay, pragmatic, revolutionary – where did they all go?

*

'It's part of the sequence, according to Baba,' Miranda says. 'Characters, they make a fuss, but what would a story be if there was no monster to defeat? Every epic needs some terror, and some terrorists. I'm Rama, you, Pascal are Hanuman with all your other monkey warriors – or if that doesn't fit – make Baba a hero-warrior. Then there's Indrajit – we're vulnerable to him, of course. You understand, my dear, his arrows pin us down, but not for long. Without the obstacles, the demons and the gods – there is no tale, no tale at all! The monsters are a necessary part, a challenge, the point of it – the plot. They can't be left out, or bypassed. You can't go from one to ten and leave out seven – even if it has an awkward look: – five doubles up in ten, but seven … where does that fit in? And yet – without it, you're a finger short – an index too! It's a little mystery, you must accept … like you must realize, that history must scroll on, it cannot move if you don't take in the seven, the anti-imperials, who're in the sequence, like it or not.… National liberation! Nationalism! Another fiction! How could you leave that out? Other people's monsters are your pets.'

'For me,' I say, 'that's all too casuistic. Some figures drop, are cancelled out, they don't compute – good riddance too! I told you – religion, fascism: leave them out!'

'Cities float away,' Miranda says. 'Species go into the river, then up to heaven, cities fall into holes, they burn, there is plague.… Always there is salvation. Guerillas love that kind of thing. We used to tell each other stories – really, there is only ever one, the same. No one expects that it will work like that down here, where here is no destiny, no hero, and no plot. No character. Destroy means destroy, and all the wonders with it….'

'You must have missed me, Miranda,' I say. 'When I was scouting for you in the world.' Trying to lighten up: I know it wasn't so, the wonders are in the tale, not here.

'You said it, Pascal,' she says. 'It's all desire. What we desired. Without an end.'

*

Conversation is not easy. I'm at fault. It's up to me to find the path, the next step … all the details such a travail means: 'Americans,' Miranda says, 'they alone don't have a story, an epic. They think they *are* it. How banal! Their bears and wolves – they've an immensity of them, they turn them out like cakes or buns – and not one of them speaks, or tells a joke, helps a granny, backs a hero, let alone they make an army, conduct campaigns. They don't fear death – not yours, not mine. We'll have to fight them, Pascal, the Americans, even if there's only two of us that's left. Believe me, we shall win.'

She is convinced, she sweeps me along with her – 'This abandoned parched expanse,' she says. 'Enslaved blacks working in the beetle pits, such horror – we shall arise, and train, and come out like battalions of lions….'

'They'll lock us up,' I say. 'France too – no longer what it was. They're all afraid, afraid they'll disappear, that in the night someone will creep into their bed, and turf them out and next day – they'll be nowhere, and someone else, who speaks good French, great grammar, is in work, will take their place…. France will appear the same, but really – changelings will take over, it will be a simulacrum.... No politicians, for sure: no liberators, no dissent ... no one will take refuge there....'

*

'I'm with you all the way, Miranda,' I say, 'though sometimes, you talk wild.'

'I like needling you, Pascal,' she says. 'It's got so boring here. You're an old slug, so dutiful. Once you'd have taken Sami's cash without a qualm....'

She's sent Baba away. 'Baba was no answer for us,' Miranda says. 'Someone we both desired, once, not now....'

'Is anyone a solution?' I ask, amazed. 'To what question? What would a solution look like? Our question is "what next"?'

'In the movie, Baba walks into the crowd, no questions asked,' she says.

'That's correct,' I say. 'As it should be.'

'Our Syrians and Kurds,' she says. 'Nothing they did, will do, should be questioned. Sudanese, Rohingya....'

'I wasn't here,' I say. 'But yes....'

'Not enough,' Miranda says. 'I want to be questioned. On behalf – of everybody. To take on everything. Me alone, my shoulders, my personal guilt – my desire, if you want. To bear witness and seek justice for injustices suffered and multiplying ... indiscriminate, the bombs, the killings.'

'You want redress, at any cost,' I say. It sounds weak.

'I'm a Leninist,' she says. 'You're a Gramscian. Delightful, soft as fondant, but wrong. A mistake. Wishful imagining.

'I want to win, and stay winning, not to be so nice I might get another try, and no hard feelings.'

'You're not alone....' I start.

'Not enough,' she says. 'Struggle. With anybody's money, and any holds at all.'

'I was with you, Miranda,' I say.

'Not enough,' she says.

How could that not be true? Enough – there never is.

*

'Did you give Baba money?' I ask.

'Certainly not,' she says. 'No one is paid for their desires. It would bankrupt the world.'

'Baba's wooden foot,' I say. 'You didn't mention it. A load, it seems, slipped and fell … a bullet … a brown bear.…'

'Certainly, it's not a sex toy,' she says. 'It's an honourable loss.'

'An accident,' I say. 'We can't forge ahead on those. We must hook on to a flow, a tide. Instinct. Even an appetite for one another – a hunger ... Baba – entirely a prosthesis – added excessively, like in black-jack – busted, dealer takes all.'

'We can't compare tattoos,' she says. 'With no one here seeking my support – sure, we must amuse ourselves. In any case, my skin can't take the ink. They etch the symbols on my face – lips and brow, hands, wrists, and feet. In the morning – it's all gone. Absorbed or extruded.'

There's a bubbling.

'We can get high on this.…' she says.

It's a tureen, big enough to hold a pair of seething twins.

The brew … looks like chanterelles, an intimate scent, overpowered by slices of boars' liver, roasted, with rosemary.

'I pass,' I say. 'The roads are full of them. Coming here – boars. Out of control.…'

She laughs, 'When was anyone in control of boars?'

I laugh too.

'How they hate us, Pascal,' she says. 'All of them, the animals, the birds, the insects, the marine things – hate us, fear us, dread our presence. It should be a lesson. We don't understand, it seems.

'It's an immense hatred, constant.'

'The tattoos,' I say, 'you aren't Berber. Of course they wouldn't take on you.'

In a small shed, too low for a human to stand up in, there are stacks of fat black bodies, small, but not tiny, not by any means. Smoked boars go very dark. I don't know what will become of them when we have left – it seems a waste, a terrible waste....

*

'We invaded everywhere,' Miranda says. 'No one was interested. Nothing has changed. We tarted up our promises – still, no one was interested. We were ghosts. We must find another approach, Pascal ...'

She's right. If we want to change the world, understanding it – or, rather, ourselves – is no use, no use at all. Try something else, absolutely.

I linger by the bus stop, undecided.

Sami's here, waiting to depart: 'Miranda took the money,' he says. 'She promised. Do you believe she's ready to farm bugs?'

'Those roaches are determined,' I say. 'I never saw a human get the better of one.'

1

Hope

The lone goose is rather small, though his voice, rarely used, is heard all over the archipelago.

He must have tired, seen the water underneath – dropped out of the formation. 'What the hell, I'm finished....'

It's just a lake.... He has a court; two white ducks, some stragglers. He's the top guy.

Sea birds get blown in ... a flamingo, from a private zoo, drops by: move on or die. Die here.

We try to be civil to each other, Vanessa and I – then, why the hell bother, we stop. We ignore the other, we ignore ourselves. What comes between us – is China. An immensity.

'Can you live in their hegemony?' I ask myself. Of course. You adapt, or you're just sad. It doesn't mean that things will work like under our capitalism – where there's indifference. What does the new regime mean, the new capitalism? You might be considered, taken notice of, given what you can't do, don't want, have you live bad but not the usual bad you've always made to live in, learned to support. Or else – there'll be big battles, postponements, less of everything, tougher lives.

We could be dead, long before anything at all.

'Your story, Maxim,' Vanessa asks. 'The power play. Did you tell anyone but me?'

'Of course,' I say. 'Sorting out a place – being invited in, or not, it's a big prospect. It often happens, even when you don't need years to be a resident. You float to the top, when you feel real light. It happens everywhere – you have the story, the determination, you're unknown but know everything. Of course; I told everyone, anyone who'd listen, or who pretended to.

'I know what must be done and I can do it. Is that the power? Is that the most we get, that seems like ruling the whole world but really almost zero, maybe you manage a little war, a movement, an idea, or – likely – zero? We're unalike – you're sensitive and flexible. You can be satisfied in mediocre situations. I'm demanding – I never get what I would want, and I give less than anybody needs. Less and less.'

'I think you have the power,' she says. 'You can convince. It's like your hobby – no one but you would be enthusiastic for it, but you are obsessed, no one can doubt you. You'll do it, you have done it, it's being done. There is no tense for intelligence, what happens and what might – they are the same, except what hasn't happened is something you can arrest. What you want and what you can – they're bound together, like ivy on a sapling. It's theory, until you try it, but it's as if you already have, and made a stir. As if you are the big chief, with a bodyguard and special forces and intelligence, where all the others are discredited – just as they always are. You have it all, to be the big one, the guy with the answers, the solution we don't trust but we follow you anyway....

'But – you didn't do it, and you'll suffer for it as if you did, and even had success. There's no way to get rid of something that you haven't done – no trial, no commission, no condemnation, nothing to justify – what didn't happen…'

'But might well have done,' I conclude, dismayed.

'There's people paid to listen, and if what they hear is plausible, grandiose, exaggerated and subversive – you suffer for it all your life, if life you have to live it still,' she says. 'You're an idiot,' she goes on, without affection. 'It's that you're a suicide without the motive. You've destroyed yourself by being plausible, by understanding what might be.... And you've done nothing! Nothing for yourself, or anyone.'

'I've done everything,' I say, 'been caught, and not stopped. Doing? Vainglory? Imagine the soldier ant, in uniform and medals, who says, 'Improving the condition of the soldier ants. That has been my mission.' It's laughable. Here, they manage a campaign while over there, they march straight up the volcano and millions are swept away in rivers of molten rock....'

'Trite,' she says.

'My father had a family,' I say. 'Mountain people – pistols, daggers, clothes faced with silver – right back they went, earlier than photography, back to watercolours, the names slipped back from generation to the previous, fathers and sons indistinguishable, the same name, same graveyard – "had issue".... Brothers and sisters, spreading out – marrying, having issue, the names like a garland round a tree. Issue? Me, but I had no family, I'd fallen off the branch. I lived on the plain, alone, with no relatives, not that I missed them, not if they were all like him, them ... the boss father – I was small, couldn't defend myself, so you dig a hole, a burrow. It's good, it works. You can move around – if there's danger, just dig another hole.

'A guy took a shot, I remember – a cop fired back. Rebellion, resistance, at bay against repression, order, revenge. That is the easy way of titling the scene. You can't look it up, not anywhere – all ephemeral, but what you do look up, it's full of silhouettes like those two – the peasant and the cop. Denied by everyone, it never happened.'

'You weren't defenceless,' she says. 'You made up another tale. You were determined, that's all. You didn't need a father or a family – not ever. You were modern. Self-made, and self-contained. Discardable, of no account, "do not trace", "leaves no mark".'

'I know you, Vanessa,' I say. 'You want power, the power you think I have usurped. Power handed over by someone to another – isn't worth a spit. I told you – I'm scum. Why would you want my dirty job? Of course – you're reactionary, you're hopeful, no sense of humour, no wry face as we go on our slide and gather speed.... Take all you want, of power, and I'll be there to trip you up.'

*

How sad, the dark. But when you think – there must be night, or else no earth revolutions, no other side to anything, everybody walking up and down and talking all the time. But at least you know the dark is bad, bad for you, you can't even hide in it, even your shine shows you up – your nose, a bald head. They say there's wonders in the night. It isn't true. There's predators – and the owl of wisdom, naturally, always too late, always questioning, always unsure and self-obsessed – 'who? Who? To who, who to?' No idea. Not even 'who whom?' The owl, if he exists, is unseen until you feel his beak – a sensation you can't communicate, not ever.

*

You're not in luck, not when you end up here. You can't say it's chance. There's not much interest in that 'why it happens' – it's choices and mistakes, choices enforced and adding to the ensuing mistakes, the preceding ones. Of no interest whatsoever – there's no way at all to correct what's been done, to rethink what will be done.

War and peace, over and over, no divorce between those two.

Curiosity killed the cat – how far can curiosity take you or anyone? Or wounded pride, or arrogance? Desire? Want a bigger garden? Full of weeds?

No one wants to know, because they'll find out soon enough. The truth – not welcome here. It's coming, though. Meantime, what people want, apart from cash, is trees and hope – contemplating oaks or grass, or cats. It all gives hope.

1

Stop

Stop. It's easy. There's nothing hypothetical. No 'then what?' No one knows about after, no one at all, never. Useless. Now, you just stop, that's all. And even if they make you go on, go back to work – it's not the same. First, it's been for money to continue doing it, the work. You sell your life, your soul, if you think you have one. Then, you've stopped: so, you're punished. After the force, the beating or the threat – it's gangster rule. Your work pays you for your protection. A racket.

Easy work, that everybody wants, well paid, with power. And as for all the rest, we take what's open to us. The union – hides our fears.

The General Strike. It's always fascinated. It solves the problem of a revolution, who decides, who leads, what next.... You won't go on with how you are, you all agree – and everybody stops – except the soldiers and the cops. They make you work – but they don't know beans; can't drive a train or paint a ship or heft a scythe. Next – what happens, is instinct, nature. Solidarity, you hope. If not – then not, and patience.

You try it once – then, if it doesn't work, forget it! Long ago – along the Appian way, the crucified strikers showed the bosses don't give up, they will play hard, much harder than you do.

*

By the time what is written here was written down, many sorts of birds, of mongoose lookalikes, are no longer in existence. By the time what is written here was written, this sort of writing too had gone extinct; writing about the industrial workers in the rich world, and the history they might have made.

The revolutionary miners danced on copper bar tables and their comrades threw black powder under their nailed boots: the spark, *Iskra* ... Bang or *phut.* The idea – that you could stop and everything would be utterly transformed, was spotted here and there – in Ireland, the old Yugoslavia, in Canada, in mountains, down in mines…. Every strike, however small and ineffective – there's the dream, the mirage … 'if we all did this, everywhere, the world would be transformed, all power would be ours….' The big one, the One Big Union…. Spotted like those rare pigeons, or great auks. The Stop. It went extinct, not written about, although if you believed in it, the belief was, if not enough to do it and succeed, enough. One bird lives, and it's enough, it's not extinct, the whole species is there, singing, squawking.

A single bird – to beat extinction, it's impossible, and if the song is stopped, it's impossible to start it over. It won't have worked, the wrong message. It's the way it goes, for almost everything. If we were all free peasants, stopping wouldn't work. We'd starve. But mostly, we aren't peasants and not free, and when you realize this – the great change, why it didn't work – it starts to haunt you. Haunts me. A ghost. It went extinct.

*

There's those who work, now, and the intermediaries, who think they're the bourgeoisie, who tell the workers where to go, what to do. Where to load, and what, where to deliver….

Finance, invention, trust, guidance and governance – they're flown on sprites, Ariels: they move the cash, the arms, the soldiers, round the globe. Above them, above everyone, people – maybe there are lots of them – have a project: being top. It's catching, wanting to be top, like wanting to die in your own bed. Staying top, staying alive, staying anonymous or staying loved.

*

A hundred years ago, anyone who shared a house, a room with anyone – was photographed. I have the pictures still – an arrangement of bigs and littles, ancients and infants. Sometimes, the servants, with their apron. And when they die, the photos pass to whoever finds the album. Neighbors. The groups, the family – they can't be strikers. I can't believe they are. More likely – they were casualties. All trucked off, to the packing factory, the abattoir, that produces nothing at all. Just smoke. Trenches – you fought in them, and conveniently they were graves, already dug.

*

'I'm down to speak,' I tell Francine. 'I was drunk. I said I was a libertarian, and now … I'm stuck. "The right to smoke crack"…. "*Right!*" – it seems to me it means there is a law and punishments…. A balance struck, a remedy proposed … Besides – if you smoke crack for long, you're much reduced. Is that a freedom to diminish what you are, your reaction, action? It's a paradox – your right to be diminished, taken into care. It happens so – is that what I must propose?'

'You said you'd do it, so you must,' she says.

Another paradox … saying, seems it isn't doing something….

'You'll meet people here that count….' she says.

'And they'll discount me,' I tell her.

'Say you've changed your mind,' she says. 'You have a right to smoke, but you're against it, as it counters what you stand for. Freedom, not rights, and no self-harm. Maybe they'll discard you, look for someone else. A real libertarian….'

She laughs.

Francine was a window – I looked through her, tried to fly through, and broke a wing. That'll teach me, but it doesn't. You're always on the wrong side, eyes made for distance and small rodents – you can't measure up to someone quite like you but who knows your sort. A sort all over, the world full of you, who look quite like her – all colours, all beliefs and none. Best stay your side of the glass, even if he breaks himself, trying to get at you. That's what they do. Don't be fooled. Why should she stay around – the world is full of you, Maxim, you cocked it up, everything you tried to do – brute ugliness. That's what she said; Francine.

*

I was drunk – again. Another time. We had a wedding, like they do in nature. A mating, coupling. How they struggle, both of us – my feathers puffed up like pillows stuffed with peacock plumes. It's not to reproduce – what do I know about raising chicks, or thrusting through the shell? Suppose we're an ostrich couple – the ostriches pool their eggs, a monstrous omelette…. Francine felt it was all grotesque –

'I played a whore in the theatre – it doesn't mean I like sex much,' she says. 'I love my husband too … he hated me, I'm boring – I know things more complicated that he could understand. A mismatch….'

'It's bigamy?' I ask. 'Polyandry. Him and me, in the outhouse, waiting for a call? Tonite's your night! Not in parts of China, and Tibet. Nesting, pairing – all shapes and sizes, almost everywhere, all the time, with anyone who comes to hand, me – multi-coloured, the females grey and critical … don't enjoy the sex, and besides, who's impressed with dancing, strutting, making my shirt-front a balloon, shaking my tail … Do I have children? Ours?'

'Yes, there's children,' she says. 'Not yours. But ours.'

'My conclusion's this,' I say, I'm still quite drunk: 'Look at the rats. They're communists. They look out for each other – they eat shit, but they have lovely coats, they're dirt poor, live in it, all kinds of filth, and die in it. We – you – have money, but you've acne, dandruff. We humans took the wrong turn somewhere, somewhere at the start….'

*

It's a relay – I could have jogged for ever with Francine. Then, Tabitha came next in the plot: a challenge, we would fail, no doubt, to reach an end, but you look for what might last, even if it's wrong, humiliating.

'I have to work out what kind of animal I am,' Tabitha says. 'It's a puzzle. I seem made for something I'm not into. Why with you? – am I a dog not taken out, a cat who makes pies, lives in a garden? In a shed?

'You – you seem to have no purpose. You do what's been printed out, you don't enjoy it. Are you rewarded? What would sufficiency be for you, for all of us? What's your life worth, and what's it for? You're drunk like bears are, or maybe woozy like those sea-lions – always fighting and blubbery….'

'I have no answer,' I tell her. 'You're right about me, I'm sure. But animals – many have handicaps even when they're at their peak – like unicorns. They're close, but they aren't horses, though in every other way, that's how they look: it's the horn, Childe Harold's fanfare. A poisoned gift. It makes you hide, deeper and deeper in the trees.... Innocence – what a handicap. I think of prickly animals, who must be very very prudent with each move and cuddle-up, or those who have a terrible smell they might let off if they're not concentrating. Hedgehogs, and scorpions – then there's the mantis, not made to found a happy household....'

'My species, not yours, that's the issue, my friend. It's more serious, tracing where I belong,' she says, closing the subject with a shrug.

'Those departed,' I throw after. 'The creatures who're no longer, as a group, together with us. We should in some way show regret, and honour them with rites and lamentations. How they were let down by environments and evolution. How they struggled, each of them, without support and information. What a fate....'

Tabitha casts this aside. No tears – they don't convince, not mine, not hers.

'You say it's drink,' she says. 'But it's your other version of yourself, jumping in and out of your skin. You can handle it, her, for years, and then she'll kill you. You can converse with her. Mostly, she doesn't answer back, just wants more of you. She pretends to bring you love. Self-love, my dear.

'It doesn't bother me, I'm quite indifferent. Humans are specialized in that; indifference comes easy now – we've evolved into it. Your head – air and dreams – that works approximately, but quite enough. There's crowds who're there correcting your mistakes. You're right – time, the tickytock – that lives on and on, and sees us all dead and stumbling, memories shot, legs a-tremble – that is the most of life we'll ever know. If time's not immortal – we shall never know – it strikes the hour when we are dead....'

'Genes, Tabitha,' I say. 'They are spores, we pick them up in our shoes, our ears ... horizontally transferred. They don't know time – just leaping in and out. The mushrooms – they twist everywhere, bind us together until we unspool, drop out of the net. The cosmos walks through us like a cloud, like a herd of pigs. We are connected, we are everyone and no one. Not much is up to us – we are an envelope, open to invisibles, and organisms that jump into us, ride us like horsemen do.... We don't even, each of us, have our own time. We're clusters of enormities, of vastnesses in which we're only blebs and blobs – working their time to great effect, while we are struggling on – against our premature decay, our memory loss....'

'It's not like that at all,' she says, fascinated by the possibilities. 'The key is not the singular. Not the generalized individual. Some places have had modernity for two millennia, are states and nations without nationalities.... Culture – that's died here, spread thin on everyone like margarine, a skim of fever-sweat – in other places is the honey, thick plasma that helps them speak and understand ... unchanging product, new every season, the flowers, the grasses always re-inventing. The melodies of bees, their recipes, the dance before the hive, the building skills of termites ... recognizing who we are, what we can do....'

'Speak and understand,' I say. 'We all do that, it's unavailing.... The truth, the plausible – the codes, the boss – it's all a box we fit well into, a box the same for everyone, it makes a pile, there's uniformity of scale, if space gets short, there'll be a box of boxes. The truth, the code we live by – trivial.... We're fitted into strings of time, like flies on sticky scrolls, we died, waving our many legs … from the first day we wave goodbye to younger selves … the buzz goes on.… Why, Tabitha, why?'

'We see things in the same way,' she says. 'We understand each other's pathways. Fuck it! It's exasperating. I hate it, I hate you, I hate myself, my bottled self you party on each day, and the self I thought that I alone see in the shower or in the tryst – naked and unknown, but known instead, polished off, digested all the time by you, my unique beauty gobbled in my nest.…'

'It's Jung,' I say. 'Treated so bad, he became mischievous. They thought he was a dunce. He wrote about the need to add a one to one to make a larger one, a monster person, satisfied, complete. You and the necessary other, the complementary person, who might supply the qualities you lack, what you should seek.

'That is a remedy for arguments and separations. Search out someone unlike you, that you must live with? Lunacy! So, that, you avoid. You look for someone like yourself, your interests, your ways of thought … that too, a recipe for conflict, even murder. Eternal competition, search for deficiencies and flaws. My singularity – singing my song, picking my nose.…

'There is no happy landing, no way to fall from solitude and be picked up by … who? The goddesses are all vindictive – think of Artemis, her fixation on what is most dear to her and unlike you, her worshipper … the bears, the deer. She loves what preys on what she loves.

'Venus is worse – a prayer from any supplicant will send her into passion, on to her casting couch with some new victim, besotted, horny, empty as a trumpet … ripe for tormenting and betrayal … being dumped.…'

'I'm many things you haven't dreamt,' says Tabitha. 'The social question. I am linked by drones and my computers –

everywhere.... To bidonvilles, to deserts and to swamps, to methane lakes, lands going pink or white with salt and alum. I track the columns – refugees, militias. For you and me – I care not a minimum. For people truly suffering – I follow them, I'm documented, my eyes are needle-sharp....'

'You could do archaeology too,' I say, much enthused. 'Saving all the sieving and the dust....'

I do not say – we all beam in on drones to watch the sufferings. We switch on and zoom and zoom, and if we're in the mood, we send our drones to drop a bomb, elect some guy to do it for us, scatter-shot, drop in on any likely group or ceremony....

No, I don't say it. I forbear. But as you know, and she knows too – what I think is evident.... There is no mystery left except ... who we invite, to creep up the back-stair, the fire escape, and hope it's sex they bring us, not the kidnap or the bible thump.... The other mysteries are on the calendar, they're priced and valued. Some we should survive, in others – we waver, we're in doubt. The causes of our own extermination – some at our own hand, others by cosmic rage or microscopic entities: – all on the agenda. The future – has already had its autopsy – there is no testament, no relics to bequeath. The killers are the victims, trials would be irrelevant....

*

'"Stop?"' she asks. 'Spontaneity, organization improvised? Poor dears – the species can't do that! It's malleable, it has no legs, no reservoir of breath. A setback, blacklegs, yellow-dog accords – and down it crumbles. The strikes are broken – then, into the trenches, waving flags.'

'That's not true,' I say. 'We don't know who, why and when....'

'I grant you,' she says. 'You got caught in a war where you knew no one, and it was a modern war, like in the eighteenth century. All about you, who didn't count or understand, and about what other people you didn't know, what they told you. No grand picture, just ebb and flow. No memory except not wanting any.

'That's you – one person caught in the net, like they all were, like we all are, have been – except: other people have other people. You're unique. You have no one, don't suffer for anyone except yourself, and yet – you know you aren't the story. War. For you, a mystery. Why did it happen, why did it fail to end? All you wanted was an end. Other people knew it would end, and it did not. It never has. Not that one, nor in general. It's a forest of burning trees – you run through them like a torch, flame strapped to your tail – or you stay and try to save your hut.

'You run, you've no hut. Run far enough, and you come to the end of any forest. Not this one.'

'Of course, I only see what everybody does, see what there is,' I say. 'Then, it gets my twist, my imprint. ...'

*

'Friends,' I say. 'Friends who have Pig Wars, so-called friends and tutors who destroy indigenous industries – and they're your friends and allies. They bring in a market, they say: more competition, and you flounder – you've been beaten, so what next? Cannons and trade, colonists and migrants – the suffering is coming, known, discounted. Suffering is what those native guys deserve, the masters make the sacrifice to enforce the rules. It's modern, logical. Reason is the most aggressive of all powers.

'Use the cash you've made, Tabitha ... buy something, buy someone else.... Follow the history, follow raison d'état, follow success and adaptation. Survival is the key. I'm not a friend, I know. I wanted one, but I'm not my friend for myself, still less for you. Alas, between us war is always present, the hooded bird who stands eternally ready on my wrist.

'Its twin – on yours.'

'I know,' she says. 'You're scum, but not benevolent scum. You're not impurity – you're an additive, alien, funneled in. If things turn out for you, and your side wins – it's not to make the sad ones happy.'

'Everybody grumbles, Tabitha,' I say. 'Millionaires more than any. I bring not peace but discipline, my order. Exactly what I want; what doesn't irritate me.

'What you, Everyman and Everywoman, call your freedom is infantile, unproductive. It's play, passing the time and making you feel you've cash to throw around. I want to see you suffer, all of you, especially the docile and the would-be good.'

'There's only you,' she says. 'You're my Medusa, my petrifying shield. I'm destitute. I'll bet it's not for long, but for the while.... As for your autocracy – I'm intrigued, I'll listen to you, be impressed. Maybe you're right....'

'It's not about what's right,' I say. 'It's keeping to a course, and dodging rocks. We must arrive somewhere – the table, the board-game's set up so you do. Avoid the cold extremities – to east and west, you'll find a port. It's small, the board, the atlas. Whoever designed it wasn't interested in variety, still less in fun. Land where there's goods and everything that's bad for you – and then set off again. That is the game – except, I never play. The gaming is a metaphor, the deadly one, because we're mortal, win or lose the end is just the same – for everyone....'

'This is easy,' says Tabitha. 'Puffing yourself, in front of your lover. Who's convinced?'

'I have no side,' I say. 'My side, if it exists – has me. It has no affection, no loyalty – my partners are the first to dump me, string me up, rig a trial and hollow out a cell. It's good. It's right. And will there be a call for me? I doubt it. I'm poison, I have drunk myself, my time is up already – and it's good. All good.'

'Your character,' Tabitha says. 'All anger. And surrender – in waves. Mine – desperation, and resignation – in billows. Not a good prospect for sex together … we're both indifferent anyway, that's our modern aspect. The rest – is primitive, and permanent.

'There must be dances, useful for burning off your anger. But we're used to wearing shoes quite unreliable, unsuitable for chassé-ing in, and changing moods.… Bare feet required. Make it a law, the first, the basic, one.…'

*

'You can reduce it all,' I say. 'To spontaneity. The spontaneous is the explosion – all the ingredients, the pain, resentment – all that's been present all your lives. Organisation is the minimum. But after the big bang – there's consolidation needed. That's where it all goes sour – the army, the big boss, the party, the philosophers march in … and me, somewhere outside. That's where can I step in, and take command. And there the race begins.'

'We're established. As a pair, we're hybrids – rarely found in nature when the sizes and the appetites are similar,' Tabitha says, persisting with her own discourse. 'We're incompatible. There's drama there, and we can add to it, like an opera – with servants – which we can't afford – and lovers, relatives, and bosses. We've experience in dodging those. So, back at the start – a troubled pair. And where, Maxim, might the call come for you to blunder in – where will it come from?'

I dodge the question. The workers' revolution? They stopped, and got more pay. A little. Some were fired, work was re-organised. They'd fired their shot – they were bought off. Easy. And on and on. Some were promoted, some got jobs as union bosses. No more work. And that, Tabitha, was the end, and it's the end over, and over.

'You must theorise, and make it different,' I say. 'Make something else entirely, that no one can imagine what it will be, when it starts and finishes. And take the credit for whatever happens!'

We contemplate that.

'You need something like the military,' I say. 'Where they shoot you if you disobey. Or aren't successful or loyal enough – even if you lose. A band of brigands, always starving. You can go anywhere, and not prosper. There's mercenaries, there's charities, there's world organizations, that no one knows who you are or why, or where you end up. Go anywhere, no one knows you, remembers you, identifies your accent or your powers.

'You need to know the difference – sheep and goats. That's enough.'

*

It's not ambition, it's doing this particular thing in a particular way. You end up bad, you know it: it makes no difference.

'It's old stuff,' Tabitha says: 'It's all bureaucrats and cops, and soldier-boys.'

'There's thousands like me now,' I say. 'No one discusses, no one has read a book or made an argument. Evcryone is different, alone, a soloist, it seems there is no common ground, but each will do what must be done. To make people move, you have to be sure of certain things – they eat, they learn, they work, they train, they work things out. That must be fixed. Then they can do things for themselves, and get rid of anyone who stops them, and I am there to tell them they are right. When they are, of course.'

Condottieri. Everywhere is Italy.

*

'I can't shorten the days,' I say. 'Or lengthen winter, if that would be good. But – less growth? I can surely manage that!' I laugh. 'After late capitalism – comes early exhaustion. We manage everything, and pledge our future. Suppress protests and take out loans. We're pleased to find someone thinks we have a future – but remember, if anyone exaggerates, finds a way to have us dig and weed, or chase us out – "Stop!" I'll say. I can prolong life. Anyone can, for almost everyone, if they take the measures. You don't have mates, friends, comrades. All's up to you. No good to say, "someone has to do what is required as no one will, unless it's you".'

Not for a collection, or to have more slaves, more zombies, who believe my fable, or dream that they do, that it's true – not for my stables, my palaces, my hunting lodge, my scrip, my mausoleum, my faith, my blasphemy, my red coat with the frogs – just to do what should be done, come what may. And what may come – we know exactly, if no one else does.

'Being able to hand out death – it tempers one's own fear of it. In the street – it's never certain – it means you must consider someone else, hurt them, applaud them – maybe consider their well-being. Their ill-being. It takes a weight off you. There's so many different ways to make people suffer – delay the permit, blacklist them, produce the false accusation – and there's the maelstrom, the helter-skelter in the demonstration.... It should be the bad ones who risk. But I'm not supposed to be a bad one. I risk, so we suppose – everyone can be at risk.... It's not by chance it happens, but you can always avoid the dodgy places. To survive – don't sign anything, don't conspire. Don't have friends, don't use code. Don't stash away a pistol to protect your innocent friend....'

'You're really trivial,' Tabitha says. 'Now we see it. Your lack of discrimination. You're a bearer of uncertainty – your principle.'

'I'm disappointed you think that,' I say. 'I know I'm not unique, but ... chance? It's that I'm betting on?' I really *am* disappointed.

'Try thinking about what winning means to you,' she says.

'I have,' I say. 'If you think too much about it, it slips away, and there's nothing left at all.'

'Up and down, hot and cold,' Tabitha says. 'You can sit here and it's all there, in your power. It wouldn't matter to you, not at all – not who they are, or might be – people cut down in the protests. To you, it doesn't matter if there's no one at all who has to suffer. For you, the suffering of others has no value, it doesn't signify, it is a *vulnus*. Not at all necessary....'

'It would be a failure,' I say. 'The point is to do what everybody needs and wants. True – it simplifies them, and what I need to do....'

'Suppose it isn't possible?' she asks. 'Just – you fail.'

'Then it's down; cold, sad,' I say. 'But everybody knows those movements, going down ... the sensations.'

'You'd do anything to avoid all that,' she says. 'But then – you'd collapse the world.'

'The world has that potential, naturally,' I say. 'Can I show it? Do it? I'd only give a jog – other people would do the pushing and the undermining – you can't blame me for the vulnerability of everything. If it can change, it must have the ability to disappear. You must believe in the inevitable, or else there's no time, no death, no evolution, no end to anything. I show you what you know.'

'These are imaginings,' she says. 'Stamping them on reality – proves nothing, but it's horrible. What can happen – don't look! It's terrifying. Some people think they can swell up, become great, in space. In nothing. Be modest, get help, almost everybody has an idea of how they'd like things all to be.'

'Then I needn't do it,' I say. 'My power. Someone else can demolish all they see and engineer it up again. Words don't belong to countries. If they call me, I'll pretend not to understand. I believe in geography, but not in maps.'

'I'll punish you,' she says, 'But I am thankful you didn't junk the world.'

*

Stop! Do it: say it. A hundred worlds must hatch, would need to be fed, instructed. Instead – there's too much fear. You put your foot out, as if to land on a new world, your discovery, your wish, a first step towards a strange new existence, to settle … a world where you have all the power – but instead, the gesture freezes, hangs in mid-air. Be careful – if you don't take your chance, trying to be bold, trusting what you've made – you'll end up bad. Very bad. Or mediocre, like the flies that circle round the light until they drop, are swatted.

Most things last longer than Tabitha, and me – but you peg it out, a length, a precise distance, time to be spent with other persons. Then it's done, fixed, and that's the satisfaction, such as it can be.

Most countries also have a distance they will go, so long you can't be fussed to peer and see where the horizon might finish up. We know what must be done, and we shan't do it.

Stop! Say it – and do it.

About the author

John Fraser lives near Rome. Previously, he worked in England and Canada.

www.ingramcontent.com/pod-product-compliance
Lightning Source LLC
Chambersburg PA
CBHW020550310726
48979CB00008B/1161/J

* 9 7 8 1 9 1 4 9 3 8 1 6 0 *